'I've been doing some thinking, Julie,' Rob Kennedy said abruptly. 'And I've been putting two and two together, and maybe getting five, but it seems to me that you and David knew each other pretty well all those years ago.'

'What if we did?' Julie returned, annoyed with herself for sounding defensive. 'What is it to you?'

'Nothing at all, girl dear,' Rob returned pleasantly. 'Other than this.' Now his blue eyes were very dark. 'I like Sarah Shaw, and I'm fond of the children, and I would not like anything or anyone to come in the way of Sarah and David putting their marriage together again.'

He stood up.

'And that's enough of that. I'll walk you across the courtyard in the moonlight, and we will talk about you and me.'

It was impossible to remain angry with him, and in spite of herself Julie laughed as he took her hands and drew her to her feet.

Elisabeth Scott, who was born in Scotland and now lives in South Africa, is happily married, with four children all in their twenties.

She has always been interested in reading and writing about anything with a medical background. Her middle daughter is a nursing sister, in midwifery, and is her consultant not only on medical authenticity, but on how nurses feel and react. She wishes she met more doctors like the ones her mother writes about!

Previous Title

HEBRIDEAN HOMECOMING

GIVE BACK THE YEARS

BY

ELISABETH SCOTT

MILLS & BOON LIMITED
ETON HOUSE   18–24 PARADISE ROAD
RICHMOND   SURREY   TW9 1SR

First published in Great Britain 1990
by Mills & Boon Limited

© Elisabeth Scott 1990

Australian copyright 1990
Philippine copyright 1991
This edition 1991

ISBN 0 263 77144 X

Set in 10 on 11½ pt Linotron Plantin
03-9102-57680
Typeset in Great Britain by Centracet, Cambridge
Made and printed in Great Britain

CHAPTER ONE

THE distant town was hot and dusty, and it shimmered in the heat of the African day.

I must have been crazy to leave Cape Town, Julie thought, with a pang of longing for her beloved home town, for the mountain and the sea, and the huge sprawling hospital on the lower slopes of Table Mountain.

To think that she had exchanged all that for the chance to work in a mission hospital, hours away from even this place. And to work with two unknown doctors who hadn't even managed to be on time to meet her!

'Sister Norton?'

She turned round.

He was tall, and his dark hair was unruly. Although his features were too rugged to be called handsome, his eyes were deep blue, and his smile was warm. And apologetic.

'And what will you be thinking of me, Sister, and you left here on your own all this time?'

Irish, Julie thought, surprised, here in the wilds of the Transkei.

He held out his hand, and his grip was sure and steady.

'I'm Rob Kennedy, and if you think you've come a long way from home—which I gather is Cape Town?—then you'll know how it feels to me, and Dublin a great deal further off.'

He led the way outside, to where a somewhat battered and dusty Land Rover was parked, and put her cases in the back. Then he turned and looked down at her.

'I'm sorry I was late,' he said disarmingly. 'I was collecting supplies, and it always takes longer than you think. Do you mind if we get going right away? It will take a good three hours—I got them to fill a flask for us, and pack a few sandwiches.'

'I don't mind at all,' Julie replied with truth, for suddenly her qualms had gone, her earlier excitement had returned, and she was longing to reach Tabanduli Mission Hospital.

'I'll give you a hand up,' the Irish doctor said, and before Julie, with her usual independence, could refuse, his hands were around her waist, lifting her effortlessly on to the high step of the Land Rover. With her face now on a level with his own, he seemed to have forgotten to remove his hands from her waist.

'Thank you, Dr Kennedy,' Julie said, politely and firmly.

'A pleasure, Sister Norton,' he replied, laughter in his blue eyes.

But when he had stridden round to the driver's side and climbed in, he looked down at her.

'Since the two of us are exiles from our homes,' he said, and she was sure his Irish accent was stronger, 'surely we will not need to be on formal terms? You will be calling me Rob, and I will surely call you Julie.'

In spite of herself, Julie laughed aloud. 'You may be an exile,' she returned, 'but Cape Town isn't all that far away. But—that's fine with me.'

Rob Kennedy started the Land Rover and drove away from the small airfield, and the dusty town shimmering in the heat.

'The engine's pretty noisy—it makes conversation difficult,' he said loudly after a while, and Julie nodded in agreement.

She was glad of the chance to look around, at the

rolling grassland with very few trees or bushes, at the distant clustered settlements of thatched rondavels on the hillsides. And glad, too, to have a few unobserved—she hoped—glances at the Irish doctor.

Not really good-looking, she decided, but—yes, there was something decidedly attractive about him, and his smile was quite something. It would be interesting to find out what kind of a doctor he was, for in her twelve years of nursing Julie had met many kinds of doctors, some good, some not so good. Some compassionate and caring, some unrealistic idealists, and some who were doing a job, and nothing more. So where would this tall dark Irishman come on her private scale? And the other doctor—was he older, younger? she wondered. Rob Kennedy, she guessed, was probably a few years older than she herself was, at twenty-nine.

He turned unexpectedly then, and found her studying him, but it didn't seem to bother him, although Julie felt warm colour flood her cheeks.

'We'll stop halfway!' he shouted, and again she nodded.

When he did stop, they were almost two hours out of Umtata, the capital, where he had met her. Now they were in the heart of the rural countryside, and when Julie got out, a little stiffly, and looked around, she could see the grasslands stretching for miles.

'I like to stop here, you get a good view,' said Rob Kennedy, taking a basket from the back of the Land Rover. There were a number of clusters of the small, thatched round dwellings, and Julie could see smoke rising from many of them.

'The doors all face east,' Rob said, 'because that's the side of the rising sun, and all the good spirits.'

He set out two mugs and poured coffee into them.

Gratefully, Julie took one, and the sandwich he offered her.

'How long have you been here, at the hospital?' she asked him.

'Almost a year,' he told her.

She wanted to ask him what had made him decide to come here, to a small mission hospital in a Third World country, but it wasn't, she thought, the sort of thing you should ask someone you'd only just met.

'You've no idea how relieved I was when I saw you at the airfield,' he said unexpectedly. 'I wasn't sure what you'd be like.' And then, disarmingly, 'Because we're a mission hospital, we do sometimes get—unusual nurses.'

'I don't think there's anything unusual about me,' Julie told him, smiling. 'I'm just an ordinary nurse.'

'Not so ordinary,' the doctor replied appreciatively, and all at once, foolishly, Julie was glad she'd worn the sea-green cotton dress that made her eyes more green than grey, glad that the sunshine always brought out the hint of russet in her smooth brown hair.

Too much charm for his own good, she told herself briskly, as Rob Kennedy's dark blue eyes lingered on her face.

'I wouldn't say no to another sandwich,' she said.

'I like a girl with a good appetite,' Rob told her, handing her the packet.

'What about the other doctor—has he been there longer than you have?' she asked him.

'A few weeks, that's all,' he told her. 'But he's a married man, and a nice girl like you will not be bothering with a married man. Especially,' he added disarmingly, 'when there's an unattached fellow like me there.'

Julie laughed aloud. 'Dr Rob Kennedy,' she said, looking up at him, 'let's get one thing clear. I came here to work, to get wider nursing experience, not to look for romances with doctors, whether they're married or not!'

'I thought that would be the way of it,' Rob agreed, unabashed. 'And is that because there's someone special back in Cape Town?' His voice was casual—carefully casual.

'No, there's no one special,' Julie said.

And unbidden, taking her by surprise, the thought was there—there hadn't been anyone special since David.

'But there was someone?' Rob Kennedy asked, and somehow she couldn't take offence at the personal question, for there was nothing but concern in his eyes, as if he had seen and recognised the fleeting shadow on her face.

'Oh, a long time ago,' Julie said lightly.

Ten years ago, she realised, with surprise. Ten years since David Shaw had stood with her outside the Nurses' Home at the huge hospital where she'd been doing her training and he was a houseman. He had looked down at her and had said, quietly, that he was going back home to Durban, back home to marry the girl he was engaged to.

It hadn't been easy for him, Julie had known that, and through the lonely months after they parted she had held on to the thought of his loyalty to the girl back home, the loyalty that he had chosen to put before the love they felt for each other.

'Hey, come back!' said Rob, but his voice was gentle.

'What about you?' Julie asked quickly. 'Anyone special for you, Rob?'

He put the empty mugs back into the basket. 'My philosophy,' he said, and now his voice was as light as hers had been, 'is to make the most of whatever life offers me.'

'I've met plenty of doctors like you,' Julie told him, meaning it.

'Not only doctors, now,' he returned, and again there was laughter in his blue eyes.

'No, not only doctors,' she agreed. 'Just men.'

'The real thing,' Rob said then, and now there was a hint of seriousness in his voice, 'is that I've never yet met a girl I could be faithful to for the rest of my life.'

Julie couldn't hide her interest. 'And that's what marriage means to you? Being faithful for the rest of your life?' she asked.

He shrugged. 'Well, girl dear,' he said apologetically, 'I'm an old-fashioned fellow at heart, although you might not think so, and—yes, it does.'

So, Julie thought, amused and a little intrigued, we know exactly where we stand. The last thing on Dr Rob Kennedy's mind is marriage, and he certainly isn't the kind of man I'd ever want to marry. But it could certainly make life more entertaining, in a place like this, knowing him.

'Tell me something about the hospital,' she asked him, when they got back into the Land Rover, and although talking above the sound of the engine wasn't too easy she could see that, once he had started, there was a great deal he wanted to say, and she liked the enthusiasm in his voice.

'Well, now, you were saying you wanted to get wider experience—I think I can safely promise you that you'll find that here,' he told her. 'We have a TB ward, and a maternity ward, and a general ward, and we have a small room that sometimes has to be used as a psychiatric ward, while we are waiting to get a patient to Umtata.' He glanced down at her. 'I gather you've a few years' experience as a midwife in the townships near Cape Town?'

'Yes, I have,' Julie told him. 'After I qualified as a midwife, I worked for five years in one of the MOUs.'

He raised his eyebrows.

'Midwives' Obstetric Units,' she explained. She told him how the system worked—the clinics with the pre-natal care, the regular check-ups, and the small hospital where the mothers came to have their babies, to stay a few hours, and then go home.

'And the follow-up?' Rob asked, obviously really interested.

'Daily visits for a week, by our staff who are on District,' Julie told him, 'and then we hand them over to the baby clinic.'

'And if anything goes wrong during a birth?' he asked.

'We call Flying Squad,' she said. 'And the patient is taken to hospital, usually to Groote Schuur. Same if there's any problem with the baby.'

He glanced down at her. 'You obviously enjoyed working there,' he said.

'Oh, I did,' Julie agreed. And, without thinking, 'You see, we were all pretty experienced, and apart from emergencies we didn't have doctors telling us what to do.'

Rob threw back his dark head and laughed. 'And you prefer not having doctors to tell you what to do?' he asked, and there was a warm, teasing note in his voice that she couldn't resent.

'Not when I know as much as they do,' she returned, with spirit.

'I'll remember that,' he promised, 'and I'll keep out of your way around the maternity ward!'

He stopped the Land Rover again an hour later, and they got out to stretch.

'Not far now,' he told her, 'but I thought you looked as if you were getting stiff.'

'I was,' Julie replied, grateful to be able to move around. 'I seem to have been sitting on planes and in cars all day.' She looked up at the tall doctor. 'You mentioned that you have a TB ward—do you have much TB here?'

'Too much,' he said. 'Malnutrition—overcrowding in homes and in schools—that doesn't help. And neither does the treatment given by the *sangomas*.'

'The *sangomas*? The witch-doctors?' Julie queried, taken aback. 'I know they're still a powerful influence among the tribal people, but surely they don't treat TB?'

'Yes, they do,' Rob replied. 'They treat it with a course of enemas and emetics, which of course doesn't cure it, and before the patient either dies or comes to us he infects far too many other people.'

He felt very strongly about this, she could see, and she thought all the more of him for that.

It's a whole new world for me, she thought, and although it had taken her only a few hours, really, to fly from Cape Town to Umtata, and to drive here, the life she had left behind, the ordered discipline of the hospital, the reasonably predictable days and nights of work, seemed so very different from this world she had come to that she had another moment of misgiving. Would she fit in here, would she make the grade?

'Come on, it isn't as bad as all that,' said Rob, and the warm kindness in his voice made her return his smile immediately.

'How did you know what I was thinking?' she asked him, as she got back into the Land Rover—unaided, this time.

'You have a very transparent face, girl dear,' he told her.

He pointed out the hospital half an hour later, away in the distance. It was smaller than Julie had expected, and the squat concrete buildings were certainly not beautiful.

But the grasslands rose behind the hospital, and on the skyline there was another group of thatched rondavels. The sun had just gone down, and some of the heat of the day had dissipated.

'Well, what do you think of Tabanduli Mission Hospital?' Rob asked.

'It's smaller than I thought it would be,' Julie admitted.

'It isn't big enough,' he told her. 'We need more space, more equipment, more drugs—more of everything except patients!'

He drew the Land Rover up in a dusty courtyard. There were only a few people around, sitting waiting patiently on concrete benches.

'Relatives of patients,' Rob told her briefly. He looked at his watch. 'I'll take you to your room first—it's over here.'

Her room was small and square and functional. She hadn't expected luxury, but she admitted to herself, as she looked around, that she hadn't expected it to be quite as basic.

'Female staff on this side, male staff on the other side, strict segregation,' Rob told her cheerfully. 'Bathroom along this corridor—you'll meet the others at supper.' He put her suitcases down. 'Clinic should just be finished,' he said. 'Let's go over and get some more of the introductions done. You can unpack later.'

He led the way out of the small room, along the corridor, and out again into the courtyard.

'That's the clinic,' he told her. 'Seems to have been a quiet day today.'

An old black man with a bandaged leg came down the steps, followed by two children and a young woman. They joined the people who had been waiting in the courtyard.

'Here he is now,' Rob said, and Julie turned from watching the old man being greeted by another even older man.

At the top of the steps, there was a man in a white coat.

Julie stood still, and she could hear her own indrawn breath.

It was David Shaw.

Her David.

No, not her David. He had stopped being that—by his own choice—ten years ago.

CHAPTER TWO

THERE was no answering shock of recognition on David Shaw's face.

He knew I was coming, Julie realised, as he came across the courtyard towards her.

'Hello, Julie,' he said, and he held out his hand. 'Nice to see you after all this time.'

Often, through the years, Julie had wondered how it would be meeting David again. And now that it was happening there was a sense of unreality, that it should happen here, in this dusty courtyard outside a small mission hospital. She had thought, from time to time, that it was possible he might come back to Cape Town, back to the big hospital, and she had been prepared for that. But not here, not now.

Somehow she managed to recover, to put her hand in his for a moment, to smile into the grey eyes she had once known so well.

'Quite a surprise, David,' she said, as lightly as she could. 'Of course, all my arrangements were made with Mr King in Cape Town, so I didn't know you were here.'

Rob looked from Julie to David. 'You two know each other?' he said, surprised.

Before Julie could say anything, David spoke.

'Yes,' he said, easily. 'Julie was in her final year when I was a houseman.'

'You didn't say, when we were looking at Julie's file,' Rob said, and Julie had a momentary realisation of some hostility between the two doctors.

'It wasn't important,' David returned casually.

15

'Besides, it might not have been the same Julie Norton I'd known.'

It was almost like a physical pain to hear him say that. 'It wasn't important.' For a moment, treacherous tears stung Julie's eyes. And then, as she turned away, ready to make some casual comment on the view, the hospital, the patients—anything—she met David's eyes.

Suddenly it was as if those ten years had never been, the years they had been apart, for she knew, as clearly as if he had said the words aloud, what he was telling her.

I'm sorry, Julie, I had to do it that way. Please understand.

And she did. Of course she understood. How could he have said to Rob Kennedy, 'I know Julie Norton. She and I were once in love.' And just to say they had known each other? Couldn't he have done that?

No, of course he was right, it was better done this way, better for both of them.

'Come and meet the rest of the staff,' David said then. 'This is the staff dining-room over here.'

I should have asked about his wife and his children right away, Julie realised, as she walked between the two men across the courtyard. But it was too late now, for Rob pushed open the door and led the way in.

The dining-room, like her own room, was very basic. There were two women in the room, and a young black girl, all in nurse's uniform, and they all smiled in greeting.

'This is Sister Norton,' David told the others. 'She and I knew each other at Groote Schuur quite a few years ago. Sister Norton—Sister Nguli.'

Sister Nguli was a large African lady, but in spite of her size she moved lightly on her feet as she came round to Julie.

'I too trained at Groote Schuur,' she told Julie. 'But

many years before you were there. Dr Shaw tells me you
have worked in the MOUs. Tell me, is Sister Ntana still
there?'

'Oh, yes,' Julie replied. 'And still the one everyone
turns to in any emergency. You know her?'

'We trained together,' Sister Nguli told her. 'Then I
went on to do community health, before coming back
home, and she decided that what she wanted was to be a
midwife.'

'And an extremely good midwife at that,' Julie said,
meaning it, and somehow this link with her old life made
her feel already more part of this new place and this new
life.

'And this is Staff Nurse Braun,' David went on, and
Julie turned to meet the other woman.

'Good day, Sister, I'm happy to have you here,' Sister
Braun said, carefully, formally.

'Like me, Nurse Braun is a foreigner, and we sometimes struggle with the language—or rather with the
accent, don't we, now, Elsa?' Rob said comfortably.
'Nurse Braun, and Nurse Jansen, came to us through the
mission itself—oh, I forgot to show you where it is, just
over the hill from us—and they come from Germany.
Monika—Nurse Jansen—is the only one on duty, you'll
meet her later.'

He turned to the young black girl, standing shyly
beside Sister Nguli.

'And this is Patience,' he said affectionately. 'Patience
wants to be a nurse, and maybe next year she'll go and
do her training, either in Cape Town or in Durban.
Meanwhile, we couldn't do without her here.'

It was not, Julie thought later, an easy meal, or an easy
meeting. Elsa Braun was very correct, very formal, and
although the African sister was pleasant and welcoming,
and interested in asking Julie about her work in the

townships and in the hospital, it would take some time, Julie knew from experience, for an easy relationship to develop. The girl Patience was very shy.

And the two doctors—although they discussed the supplies Rob had got in Umtata that day, and some problems he had run into, and then what had happened in the hospital here during the day, there was a formality between them that was strange, Julie thought, for two men, probably much the same age, who had worked together in a small mission hospital for a year.

It didn't seem the right time or place now, to ask David about his wife and his children. She had gathered that David, as the senior doctor, lived in the small house that was a little way up the hill above the hospital, while Rob lived in a room that Julie guessed must be much like her own. So probably David was eating here tonight only because she was here.

He hasn't changed much, she thought, looking across the table at him. Fair hair—and, beside the smooth cap of his hair, Rob Kennedy's dark hair looked even more rumpled—grey eyes. He was thinner than she remembered, but his smile was still the same.

He looked across the table at her at that moment, and once again it was as if the ten years since they had last seen each other had gone. But of course, she reminded herself, that was a foolish thought, and the less she allowed herself to think in that way, the better.

All at once she felt very tired. And needing to be alone, to face up to this realisation that she would have to handle seeing David, meeting his wife, his children, seeing just what these years had been to him.

She stood up. 'Would anyone mind if I went to bed?' she said, and with an effort she smiled. 'I don't know why just sitting around in planes and cars is so tiring, but it is.'

Rob stood up too. 'I'll walk you across,' he said. 'I want to look into the general ward in any case.'

Julie knew she had to find out about her duties tomorrow, but she wasn't sure who she should ask—David, Rob, or Sister Nguli. And it was important, she knew all too well from all her nursing years, not to tread on any toes, especially at this stage.

Rob came to her rescue. 'I think we want Julie in Maternity, don't we, Sister Nguli?' he asked. 'That was what we decided?'

The big nurse nodded. 'You have more experience than I do, Sister Norton, I'm glad to have you in Maternity.'

The stars were very clear in the sky, and now Julie could hear the silence all around them.

'It's a strange thing, now,' Rob said conversationally, 'that David Shaw did not think it worth while mentioning that he thought he might know you.'

'Well, it was a long time ago,' Julie replied.

And, as she said it, she remembered that she had used the same words when Rob had asked her if there had been someone special in her life. Would he realise that the someone special had been David? He had said she had a transparent face—had she given anything away, in the shock of seeing David again?

'I really am tired,' she said, more abruptly than she had meant to. 'Thanks for keeping me right on the protocol—I didn't want to do anything wrong.'

They had reached the door of the corridor to her room. In the clear moonlight, he looked down at her.

'We're not so hot on that as you'll have been in a big hospital,' he told her. 'But just so that you get it straight—we discuss what's to be done, David and I, with Sister Nguli, and we leave her to tell the nurses.' He hesitated. 'In a while, when you and she are more used to each other, she might appreciate a hand with the organisation and with the paperwork.'

'I'm glad to know that, and I'll just take my time,' Julie replied. 'Thanks for picking me up today, Rob—I suppose I'll see you around my ward tomorrow?'

She could hear in his voice that he was smiling, and she was pleased that the warmth she had known earlier was back.

'Oh, yes, you'll be seeing me,' he agreed. 'In fact, you'll find we all live very much in each other's pockets here, and it such a small place. Oh—breakfast at six-thirty, Julie, on the ward at seven.'

Julie went along the corridor and into her room. It looked, she thought, even barer than her first impression of it. She'd have to do something to brighten it up. But for now all she would do was unpack quickly, lay out her uniform ready for morning, have a quick bath, and get to bed.

But, tired as she was, she couldn't fall asleep. It wasn't of this day, strange and disturbing as it had been, that she found herself thinking, but of a day ten years ago, the day David had said goodbye to her.

She hadn't known at the start that there was a girl back home—Sarah—and by the time she did know she'd been deeply in love with the young doctor. And people changed, they grew away from each other, she'd told herself, surely this Sarah would understand that.

They hadn't spoken much about her, she and David, after David had told her, and Julie, so certain of their love, had felt that David must be waiting for the right time, the right way, to tell Sarah. Perhaps when he went home towards the end of his year as a houseman.

But it was when he came back that he had told her he was leaving Groote Schuur, leaving her. He'd been going to take up a resident's post in the local hospital, and marry Sarah.

Sarah had been ill, he'd told her. He hadn't gone into details, and Julie hadn't wanted to know, but somehow, over the years, she had retained the impression of a girl whose health would always be a problem, a girl who would face life more easily with David beside her.

'She needs me, Julie,' he had said, his voice low. 'I can't walk out on her now.'

She hadn't tried to make him change his mind. Partly because her pride hadn't allowed her to, but perhaps even more because she could see that his decision had been made.

And in the first bleak weeks and months without him, she had held on to the thought that it was his loyalty to this girl that had taken him away from her. And, lonely and heartbroken as she'd been, she couldn't help admiring him for that.

Not that she had spent the years since then mourning for her lost love. She was naturally resilient, and although for a while she put everything into her work before long there were other men, other friends, and her life was full and happy.

But, lying now in the darkness of the African night, Julie had to admit to herself that always, deep down, there had been the memory of David.

Somewhere around midnight she fell asleep, to awake to the sound of her alarm clock—a familiar sound, but it took her a moment to remember where she was. All the years of discipline and early rising got her to the staff dining-room at six-thirty, her uniform—white and short-sleeved, to suit the weather—spotless, her badges and epaulettes in position.

Rob was pouring coffee for himself as she went in, and he poured some for her as well. There was no sign of

David, and she was glad of that. He would, of course, she reminded herself, have breakfast with his wife and his children.

'Patience has already had breakfast,' Rob told her. 'She's so keen, she's always ready to start early. Agnes— Sister Nguli—is dieting, so she's having fruit in her room. Elsa will rush in in five minutes or so.' He smiled at her as he passed her a plate with toast on it. 'No egg today, but there's cereal if you want.'

Julie shook her head. 'Coffee and toast will do me fine.'

The momentary coolness that had been in his eyes, when he'd said how strange it was that David hadn't mentioned knowing her, had gone, and she was glad of that.

'Who do I have with me on Maternity?' she asked him.

'Patience,' he told her. 'Remember, she does struggle a bit with English, so make sure she understands.' He stood up and looked at his watch. 'We've got a fellow with an ulcer in General, I want to have another look at him—we have to decide today whether to send him to Umtata or whether to keep him here under observation a little longer.' And at her questioning look, 'If it's a matter of an operation, we send people to the big hospital— we're not surgeons. We'll deal with emergencies, and minor procedures, but we like to refer anything major. Got to watch our position, too, as a mission hospital, now that most of the hospitals here come under the State. See you later.'

As he hurried out, the German girl came in. In the clear light of day, Julie saw that Elsa was probably older than she had thought last night, perhaps around thirty-five.

'I will be quick, Sister,' Elsa said, sitting down.

'It's all right, I'll go over to my ward now—have your breakfast properly,' Julie said.

The other German nurse—Monika Jansen—had been the only one on night duty, she explained when Julie went into the maternity ward. She had in fact been on duty over all the wards, because they were so short-staffed, but Sister Nguli had been on call if necessary.

'We are quiet just now,' the German nurse said—her English was better than Elsa's, Julie noticed. 'There is only Mrs Mafana, who had her baby two days ago and will go home tomorrow, and Mrs Wilson from the mission. Mrs Wilson has diabetes, and Dr Shaw wishes to keep her in still for a few days, although already her baby he is four days old.'

Julie greeted the two patients, and took their charts from Nurse Jansen, but before she looked at them she admired the babies in the cots beside their mother's beds.

'Your first, Mrs Mafana?' she asked, and the African woman laughed.

'No, Sister, this is my fourth, and this is the daughter we have been waiting for.'

'It's my first one, Sister,' the young English girl in the next bed said shyly. 'I'm longing to get home with him, but Dr Shaw says not yet, because of the diabetes.'

Julie went back to the tiny room that served as a combined duty-room and office, and studied the charts. 'Four-hourly temps, in case of sepsis, graduated exercises,' she murmured. 'And ambulant to minimise the risk of thrombo-embolism.' She looked up at the German nurse. 'Nice to know that Dr Shaw's treatment is just what I'd do myself,' she said cheerfully.

Nurse Jansen looked shocked. 'But of course the doctor knows always what is best to do.'

Better not shock her any further by saying that doesn't always work, Julie thought. 'You go off now, Nurse

Jansen,' she said. 'Ah, here's Patience, she and I will get going now.'

The young black girl was eager to work, and eager to learn, Julie found. Although she seemed so quiet and shy, she was firm and confident dealing with the patients, and experienced, Julie could see, with the babies.

'You're very good with these tiny babies,' she said, as Patience took a bathed and changed Baby Mafana back to her mother.

'I would like to work just with small babies,' Patience told her. 'But first I must do my general training, and then I can learn all about the babies.'

With only two patients, it didn't take long to have the small ward neat and ready for the doctor coming, and by the time David arrived both the women were out of bed, Mrs Mafana sitting beside the window because she said she would have no time for sitting when she was home, and young Mrs Wilson walking up and down the length of the small ward, as she had been told to.

Julie showed David the charts, and the graph of the babies' weights.

'I think we'll let Helen Wilson go in a couple of days,' he said, when they were back in the small office. 'Because she's at the mission, we can keep an eye on her—we were pretty worried about this diabetes at one stage, now we have to check on any changes. So keep on with the temps and the movement, and call me if you need me.'

He looked down at her.

'Settling down, I hope?' he said then. Patience was changing one of the babies, close to them, so there was no chance to say any more, either for him or for her. Not that there was anything to be said, Julie reminded herself. Other than that she should ask about his wife, and his children. Because there was obviously a good chance that very soon she would meet them, for surely, with his house so close to the hospital, they would be around.

It was a busy day, and she was glad of the familiar routine of work—familiar although the place was strange. In the afternoon there was a prenatal clinic, and there were nine young pregnant women, some of them living in settlements fairly close, but two of them, she was taken aback to discover, living miles away.

'This is the hospital closest to them,' Patience explained.

'I hope they get here in good time when the babies are due,' Julie said.

'Often they don't,' Patience replied, matter-of-factly. 'What is it Sister Nguli writes then on the form?'

'BBA,' Julie told her. 'Born Before Arrival.'

Her lunchtime had been hurried, and she had seen neither David nor Rob, but when she went for dinner Sister Nguli told her that the Irish doctor had gone to see a patient up at the mission, and she didn't know when he would be back. Julie couldn't help feeling a little disappointed, for she had been looking forward to talking to Rob about her first day, about the hospital itself, perhaps to find out what had brought him here. She and the African nurse talked about some of the people they both knew in Cape Town, and then Sister Nguli excused herself, saying she had letters to write.

I should do that too, Julie thought, for she knew her folks would be longing to hear all about everything. She stood up, ready to go to her room to do this, but as she reached the door David came in.

'All alone, Julie?' he said, obviously disconcerted. 'Look, I hope you understand why I didn't say anything to Rob about—our knowing each other.'

'Of course,' she replied quickly. Too quickly, she knew.

And then, before she could lose the small amount of courage she had, she said, with difficulty. 'Your wife must find it isolated living here. And how do you manage for school for the children?'

He looked down at her. 'I thought you knew,' he said, his voice low. 'I thought Rob would have told you.'

'Told me what?'

'Sarah and I are separated. She isn't here with me,' he said.

'No,' Julie heard herself say. 'No, I—didn't know, David.'

CHAPTER THREE

AFTERWARDS, when Julie could think clearly about how she felt when she knew that David was here alone, she had to be honest with herself. Painfully honest.

She had to admit that in that first moment, as her thoughts and her emotions whirled, she could see these lost years—the years since she and David had parted—given back to her.

Immediately she was ashamed of these thoughts, angry with herself. This was a broken marriage, there were children who were no longer in the family background they had always known.

'I'm so sorry, David,' she said, not quite steadily. 'I just took it for granted that—your wife and the children were here with you.'

She had thought she could say the name Sarah, but she hadn't been able to.

He shrugged. 'One of those things,' he said.

Julie wondered if Sarah had refused to come with him to the mission hospital, so far from civilisation. But she couldn't ask him that. Not now. Not yet.

'I miss the children,' he went on, his voice low.

'How old are they?' Julie asked, and thought, how strange and unbelievable, to be standing here with David, talking about his separation from his wife, about him missing his children. And then—how strange and unbelievable to be here with David at all.

'Timothy is eight, and Clare is six,' David told her. 'They——'

He stopped, and she turned to see Rob coming in.

'Hi,' he said cheerfully. 'Left me something to eat, I hope.'

'I haven't had dinner yet,' David replied, and Julie wondered if the Irish doctor noticed the slight awkwardness in his voice—and in her own, when she said she was going back to her room to write some letters.

'Sit down and keep us company,' Rob said. 'Have some more coffee. That will keep you awake to write your letters.'

He put his arm around her shoulders, lightly, casually. And Julie, because of David beside them, because she knew now that he was here alone, could not stop herself from drawing away from him. It had been an easy, friendly gesture, nothing more, and she saw that he was taken aback by her reaction. For a moment, his deep blue eyes were darker.

'Besides,' he said lightly, 'I want to talk to you professionally.'

Julie wanted to be alone, and she felt she needed time and peace to absorb what she had just heard from David. With some reluctance she joined the two doctors at the table, and accepted the coffee Rob brought her when he and David had been given plates of steak pie and vegetables by Mrs Nzama, who ruled over the kitchen.

'I've been up at the mission most of the day,' Rob told her. 'If this hadn't been your first day, I'd have wanted you to come too, since this will be your patient. At least she will be until she's due to deliver.'

'She's not going to deliver here?' Julie asked.

Rob shook his head. 'She's forty-one,' he said. 'She's never carried a baby to term, and—well, it looks as if this time she'll make it, but we're not taking any risks, she'll go to Umtata a couple of weeks before the baby is due.'

David put down his fork and knife. 'I still think Meg

should go to Cape Town, or to Durban,' he said, and Julie could see that this was a point the two doctors disagreed on.

'I know you do,' Rob returned, and once again Julie sensed that there was some hostility between them. He turned to Julie. 'Meg Winter and her husband Steve have been with the mission for over ten years,' he told her. 'I think they've been married for about fifteen years, and in that time Meg has had three miscarriages. The last one was six years ago, so they'd pretty much given up hope of a child of their own, and last year they adopted a child whose mother died when she was born—Faith, they've called her. She's a pet—eighteen months now. Anyway, as I'm sure you know, that seemed to do the trick, and now Meg is thirty weeks, and—well, it looks as if she's going to be fine.'

'So this was a false alarm, this message today that she hadn't felt foetal movement?' David asked.

The Irish doctor's blue eyes were steady. 'I looked on it as valid when Meg was worried,' he said evenly. 'I think she'd been overdoing things, so I made her promise to rest more, and I stayed around to monitor the baby's movements. She's feeling much better now.'

'If she would agree to go to Cape Town, she could have a scan done,' David pointed out.

'She doesn't want to leave little Faith any longer than she has to—I reckon it would do her more harm if we were to insist,' said Rob. He turned to Julie. 'Meg will come down in a day or two, so you can do a check-up, Julie. I was telling her about your experience in the MOUs, I'm sure she feels you'll know much more about babies than I do.'

'She's probably right,' Julie returned. 'I'll look forward to meeting her, and little Faith.' She finished her coffee, and stood up. 'I'm going to write my letters now,' she said.

For a moment David's eyes met hers, and she knew that if it hadn't been for Rob he would have walked across the courtyard with her, in the warm African night. This was a disturbing thought, and she dared not allow herself to dwell on it. She said goodnight quickly, and went across the brightly lit courtyard to her own room.

But the letter she meant to write to her parents remained unwritten, for as she sat at the small table in her room, with her writing-pad open and her pen in her hand, she found it difficult to say, casually, that David was here. They would remember, especially her mother, how heartbroken she had been when he told her of his decision to marry Sarah. And although it was so many years ago, she knew that it worried them that in all these years there had never been anyone else as important to her as David had been.

Tomorrow I'll write, she promised herself. Tomorrow, or the day after.

Here at Tabanduli, things were very different from how it had been working at Groote Schuur, the huge sprawling hospital made so famous when Professor Christiaan Barnard had done his heart transplants.

But not so different, Julie found, from her work in the Midwives' Obstetric Units where she had worked for five years. There, the midwives carried a greater responsibility, and had much more independence, using the hospital as back-up when necessary.

Here she found that both David Shaw and Rob Kennedy were only too glad to leave the responsibility for the maternity ward in her hands. There was more than enough work for both of them in the general ward, in caring for the TB patients, in clinic work both here at the hospital and in the outlying districts. Sister Nguli recognised Julie's experience as being greater than her own in midwifery.

'But when you come to the general ward, Sister Norton,' she said cheerfully, 'I think you'll be glad to let me help you.'

'I'm sure I will,' Julie agreed, for it was many years now since she had done anything but midwifery. She was relieved that the question of division of work had been settled so easily, for Sister Nguli was so much older that it could have been difficult. From previous experience of working with African nurses, she knew that the older woman would expect professional formality for some time. But she knew, too, that it would be a great compliment if and when Sister Nguli called her by her Christian name.

The small maternity ward became much busier from her second day onwards. She had just completed her morning charts when young Patience came hurrying into the small duty-room, her eyes wide.

'This woman who comes in just this morning, Sister, the baby is going to be born. Should I go for Dr Kennedy?'

'I don't think it will be necessary, Patience,' said Julie. 'I'll have a look at her first.'

The young African woman in one of the two beds in their tiny labour ward smiled as she went in. 'All my babies come quick, Sister,' she said. 'And this is my fifth.'

Julie could see that there was no time to waste. She eased her fingers into the tight rubber of the gloves, for the baby's head was showing already.

'One push should do,' she told the woman. 'Be ready for the next contraction—right, push now.'

Gently she held the baby's head and eased it out, and

then, with a swift slippery movement, the shoulders followed, and the baby was born.

'A little girl,' she said, 'and not so little either.'

She wrapped the baby in the receiving blanket Patience held out to her, and the baby gave a loud and outraged yell.

'No problem with her breathing,' Julie told the mother. 'Patience, give Mrs Mgozi her baby to hold.'

'My husband will be very happy,' the African woman said, holding her baby close to her. 'We have four sons, and he wants so much a daughter.'

Within a few minutes there was another contraction, and Julie delivered the placenta. A big baby, and no stitches needed, she thought with pride, for there had been a moment, as the shoulders appeared, when she had thought there would be a tear.

'Right, we'll clean you and your baby up, Mrs Mgozi,' she said, 'and we'll get a message to your husband.'

'I can do this, Sister Norton,' Patience said shyly. 'Always I bath the baby, and clean the mother.'

'Thanks, Patience,' Julie replied. 'I'll see to the chart once we've got the baby's weight.'

She turned to find Rob standing in the doorway, watching.

'Nice delivery, Sister,' he commented.

'It was straightforward,' Julie replied. 'No problems.'

But she couldn't help feeling a warm glow of pleasure at the appreciation in his eyes and in his voice.

He waited while she took her gloves off and washed her hands, then walked back to the duty-room with her.

'I thought she was going to tear,' he remarked.

'So did I,' Julie admitted. 'But I pride myself on my stitching, Dr Kennedy. None of my patients are uncomfortable sitting when I've stitched them.'

'Would you have done an episiotomy, if you'd had time?' he asked her.

'I probably would,' she said, after a moment. 'This is a big baby—over eight pounds, I'd say at a guess—and the mother isn't so big—yes, I probably would have, I prefer that to risking a tear. But there wasn't time even to consider that—this baby was in a hurry.'

'Sister Nguli liked either David or me to do the actual delivery,' Rob told her. 'It's going to be a great help, not having to drop whatever we're doing to come and catch babies!' With a wicked gleam in his dark blue eyes, he glanced down at her. 'Of course, we are here when you're needing a bit of extra help, when things are maybe a bit much for you.'

Julie refused to rise to that. 'I'm grateful to know that, Dr Kennedy,' she said demurely. 'Like all good midwives, I was brought up on Maggie Myles, and she says, in her *Textbook for Midwives*, that a good midwife requires sufficient knowledge and experience to enable her to recognise normal progress, and detect deviations from the natural course. And of course when that happens, I'll send for you.' Serious now, she looked up at him. 'Where do we refer problem cases, Dr Kennedy?'

'The State hospital in Umtata,' he told her. The warm teasing had gone from his eyes now. 'But you will be realising, I'm sure, Julie, that there are many times when there just isn't the time for a patient to be taken there. So your extra experience is going to be called on over and over again.' He held out his hand. 'I'll just check the charts while I'm here, and do a quick ward round— David is setting a fractured femur, and I'm doing the anaesthetic, so I'll have to be quick.'

Quick he was, Julie found herself thinking later as she stood at the door and watched him stride across the hot and dusty courtyard, his white coat flying, but he was thorough. And never without a warm sympathy and interest in each patient.

David seemed to spend more time in the general ward, and working in the clinics, she found, but if there were clinic visits to be made to some of the outlying districts, it was more often than not Rob who went.

On these days he came back late, often too late to join the others for dinner. The German nurses, Monika and Elsa, often went up the hill to the mission itself, in the evenings, to join in church services held there, and Sister Nguli and Patience seldom lingered over meals. So it seemed to happen that David and Julie would be sitting over coffee, talking, when Rob came in.

The second time this happened, Julie was conscious of Rob's eyes moving from her to David, thoughtfully, and she was conscious, too, of a warm tide of colour in her cheeks. We were only talking, she reminded herself, and that was true. They had been talking—about people they had known and worked with years ago. So far they had both, by unspoken agreement, Julie felt, talked only of other people, never of themselves. And that had made it easier for her to write, casually, in her letter home—after a long description of the small mission hospital, of her work, of the pattern of her days—that they would be surprised to hear that one of the doctors was David Shaw. She hesitated there, but didn't say anything about his wife and his children not being with him.

Now she found herself remembering that omission, as Rob's eyes rested on her.

'I'm surprised to find you still here, David,' said Rob, as he helped himself to salad. 'You're not usually sociable in the evenings.'

His voice was pleasant and casual, but Julie saw David's face tighten.

'Julie and I are catching up on news of people we both

knew years ago,' he returned, a little coolly. He stood
up. 'But I'm on my way now. Julie, I'll look in and see
that patient of yours tomorrow, and we'll come to a
decision about these varicose veins. Now that she's had
her baby, we'll probably send her to Umtata to have
them done.'

When he had gone, Julie stood up too.

'Surely not more letters to write, girl dear?' Rob said
reproachfully. 'Or have you had enough of doctors'
company for tonight?'

Suddenly she was angry with him. She sat down again.
'You didn't tell me that David and his wife were separated,' she said flatly.

He raised his eyebrows. 'And why should I?' he asked
her reasonably. 'Firstly, I didn't know you two knew
each other, and secondly—well, separated they may be,
but I'm thinking that if they give themselves a fair chance
things will work out for them. She's a nice girl, Sarah.'

Now Julie was unable to hide her surprise. 'You know
her?' she asked.

'Oh, yes,' Rob returned, and without asking her he
poured coffee for both of them. 'She's been here a few
times, she and the children. I think they just need to get
a few things sorted out, the two of them, and their
marriage will be fine.'

David hadn't actually said that Sarah had never been
here, Julie reminded herself carefully. But somehow she
had got the impression that he hadn't seen her since he
came here. Not that there was any reason for her to need
to know, she thought.

'I've been doing some thinking, Julie,' the Irish doctor
said then, abruptly. 'And I've been putting two and two
together, and maybe getting five, but it seems to me that
you and David knew each other pretty well all those years
ago.'

'What if we did?' Julie returned, annoyed with herself for sounding defensive. 'What is it to you?'

'Nothing at all, girl dear,' Rob returned pleasantly. 'Other than this.' Now his blue eyes were very dark. 'I like Sarah Shaw, and I'm fond of the children, and I would not like anything or anyone to come in the way of Sarah and David putting their marriage together again.'

He stood up.

'And that's enough of that. I'll walk you across the courtyard in the moonlight, and we will talk about you and me.'

It was impossible to remain angry with him, and in spite of herself Julie laughed as he took her hands and drew her to her feet.

The heat of the African night enclosed them as they walked across the courtyard, and she longed for a breath of fresh air.

'We'll walk up the hill a little,' Rob suggested, 'it's cooler up towards the mission station.'

She asked him about the pregnant woman at the mission station, and he said she would be down for a check-up in a day or two.

'But we're not here to talk about work,' he told her. 'Tell me about your family, Julie.'

She told him about her father, who was a bank manager, and her mother, who had gone back to teaching when the family grew up, and was now a remedial teacher.

'And she loves it,' she said, smiling as she thought of her mother, small and slim in her mid-fifties, and always full of energy and enthusiasm. 'She says it's just as well she has her children at school, since so far neither my brother nor I look like obliging her with grandchildren.'

'She would get on well with my mother,' Rob told her, and there was enough moonlight for her to see that he was smiling. 'My sister has two, and you would think, them being the young devils they are, that that would be enough for my mother, but no, there's nothing in the world she would like more than to see me married, and raising a family, and Kathleen married and doing the same.'

He looked down at her. 'You haven't been away from your family for very long, but I haven't seen mine for almost two years, and I miss them.' He shook his head. 'I even miss the dog, and him the worst fighter any Irish terrier ever could be.'

'I miss our dog too,' Julie admitted. 'Saying goodbye to her was worse than saying goodbye to people, because she couldn't understand. She saw my suitcase, though, and she didn't like that.'

'What kind of a dog is she?' Rob asked.

'She's a Labrador,' she told him. 'Golden.'

Suddenly, ridiculously, she remembered old Tess standing in the doorway of her room, looking at the closed suitcase, tail down, ears down. And she's not young, she thought, realising this with surprise.

'Hey,' Rob said softly, 'I didn't mean to make you sad, Julie.' He put one hand under her chin so that she had to look up at him. 'Did you know that there are only two sorts of people in the world?' he said, and now there was warm laughter in his voice. 'People who like dogs, and people who don't. I'm glad you're my kind.'

Julie was never sure, afterwards, how it happened. They were standing close to each other, and Rob's hand moved from her chin and touched her cheek lightly. He moved closer, and his lips brushed hers. It was a friendly kiss, nothing more.

Or rather that was how it started out. But she didn't move away from his enclosing arms, and after a moment he drew her towards him and kissed her again. And this time his lips were warm and demanding on hers, a demand that she could not stop herself responding to.

It was a long time, she thought, before they drew apart, and she could feel her heart thudding unevenly.

'Well, now,' murmured Rob, his lips still close to hers, and his arms tightened around her.

Oh, no, Julie thought, enough is enough, and she drew back. 'I think we'd better be getting back,' she said, annoyed to find that her voice wasn't quite steady.

'And here was I thinking perhaps you weren't at all minding being kissed,' Rob said regretfully.

Remembering her response to his kiss, Julie was glad he couldn't see the flood of warm colour in her cheeks.

'Come, now, Rob,' she said, as lightly as she could, 'of course I was enjoying it, and so were you. It—it's just chemistry, after all.'

'Chemistry, is it, now?' he murmured. 'Now that's an interesting thought, girl dear.'

Of course it's just chemistry, Julie told herself later, when she was back in her room alone. He caught me at a vulnerable moment, that was all, he took me by surprise.

But just before she fell asleep she had the strange and disturbing thought that their kiss had in some way taken Rob by surprise too, and that he had been as shaken as she had.

CHAPTER FOUR

WHAT'S a kiss, after all? Julie asked herself, sensibly and reasonably.

And she was relieved to find that Rob seemed to feel the same, for there was nothing in his manner the next day to show that it had been anything more than a passing impulse.

Two people, moonlight, proximity, a moment of sympathy and closeness. A kiss was a very natural development.

And so Julie put firmly away from her mind the feeling that it had been a kiss that had somehow got a little out of hand for both of them.

But it was less easy to put from her mind what Rob had said about David and his wife. He knows both of them, she reminded herself fairly, he's seen them together. And of course it was right to hope that any broken marriage might be put together again. Especially when there were children to be considered.

What Rob had had no right to say, or even to think, was that she might do anything to make things worse between them. She had to admit, privately, that it had been something of a surprise to hear from Rob that Sarah and the children had been here, with David. Somehow that did change things, from her earlier thoughts of David here alone, with no contact from his wife, and missing his children.

Because there was a difference between a man who was well and truly separated from his wife, and a man whose wife might have reason to think their marriage could be saved.

And so Julie took care to avoid any situation where there could be anything other than a completely professional relationship with David. Even there, she saw him less than she saw Rob, for it was Rob who usually came when she needed a doctor.

As she did when the young woman came in from a village two hours' journey from the hospital. Her native name was written on her file, but she was always known, she said, as Beauty. Julie had known a few black women called Beauty—one of her earliest memories was of a large, smiling woman who had helped her mother in the house, and she had been Beauty—but this young woman, in spite of advanced pregnancy, really did live up to her name, for there was a serenity about her face that was indeed beautiful.

'Beauty, you didn't come for your check-up two weeks ago,' Julie said, checking the file. 'You should have been here.'

'My grandmother was ill, I had to look after her,' Beauty replied shyly.

'Is she better now?' Julie asked, as she began to examine the young woman. 'I hope so, because you'll be glad of help when you go home with your baby.'

She went on talking, to hide the sudden concern she felt at the baby's position. If that head didn't move. . .

'Patience will bring you a cup of tea,' she said, 'and I'll check again quite soon how things are going. This is your first baby, I see.'

Two hours later the baby's head hadn't moved at all, and she sent Patience across for Rob. Fortunately he was at the hospital, and not out at an outlying clinic, and he came back immediately with the young nurse.

Julie went to meet him, to give him the information he needed out of Beauty's hearing.

'Deep transverse arrest,' she told him. 'That head just isn't moving, and she's well into second stage. I've been monitoring the foetal heartbeat, and there are signs of distress now.'

'So it looks like a forceps delivery,' said Rob, following her through to the labour ward. He smiled down at the young woman in the bed. 'Looks as if this baby of yours needs a bit of help to come into the world, Beauty,' he said easily.

Beauty's eyes were wide and anxious. 'Is the doctor going to cut me?' she said to Julie, as if Rob himself weren't there.

'No, the doctor isn't going to cut you,' Julie told her reassuringly. 'He's just going to help the baby—you won't have to be put to sleep or anything.'

Knowing this would have to be a forceps delivery, she had everything ready.

'Kielland's forceps?' Rob asked, and nodded when he saw that she had the correct forceps ready. 'I'll need them because I'll have to rotate the baby's head while I deliver. But you know that, of course, Sister.'

This was the first delivery she had seen him do, and she had had so many experiences of seeing forceps delivery that she knew right away that the Irish doctor was very skilled. Carefully, expertly, he delivered the baby, easing it out of the position that made a normal delivery impossible.

'There we are,' he said, almost to himself, and Julie took the tiny boy from the bed. 'He might need suction, Sister.'

The baby had swallowed some mucus, and his breathing was noisy, but once Julie had suctioned him he gave a few loud yells, and then settled in his mother's arms.

'He is small,' Beauty murmured wonderingly. 'My cousin's baby was much bigger.'

'He's a fine size,' Rob told her. 'If he'd been any bigger, he would have been much more difficult for me to deliver. Patience will weigh him, and maybe he is smaller than your cousin's baby, but I guarantee he'll catch him up!'

He threw his gloves into the bin and went out, Julie following him.

'That was a great delivery, Dr Kennedy,' she said, meaning it. 'I've seen plenty of forceps deliveries, but none better done. I'm sure Beauty hardly knew what was happening.'

'I'm thinking it would be worth a cup of coffee, would it not?' Rob suggested. 'For I'll have missed coffeetime across the road there.'

Julie switched on the kettle in the small duty-room, and made two mugs of coffee.

'I'm glad you were there,' she told him, meaning it.

'Yes, you would be needing a hand with a forceps delivery or a Caesar, I'm thinking,' Rob replied, and she didn't mind the warm teasing in his voice.

'I thought of doing the advanced midwifery course,' she told him, her chin up. 'Then I wouldn't have had to depend on a doctor being around, at least for the forceps!' She looked at him, serious again. 'You've obviously had a great deal of practice with forceps,' she said.

His blue eyes were dark now. 'That I have,' he agreed. 'You'll know, of course, that forceps are used when the mother has advanced pulmonary tuberculosis, and I'm afraid there is so much of that here that I have had to do far more forceps deliveries than I would want to.'

He finished his coffee, and stood up.

'Beauty is all right, though—the village she comes from is reasonably clear of TB. Right, I'll be off—let me know when Beauty is being discharged, I'll have a look at her and at the baby before they go.'

Julie rinsed the coffee-cups.

He is a good doctor, she thought, and this realisation pleased her, for she and her friends often said that no one was more critical of a doctor's ability than the nurses who saw him at work, who worked with him. There was nothing she could fault in Rob Kennedy's approach to his work, or in his skill. At least, she reminded herself, in her own field.

Already she felt much more comfortable and at home here, but she did have to admit that there was no one on the nursing staff she felt that she could become really friendly with. Sister Nguli was always pleasant, but she kept her distance, and the age-gap would in any case make it difficult. Patience was a dear girl, but very young. And the two German nurses, Elsa and Monika, kept very much to themselves. The language was a problem, for although they both spoke English—Monika Jansen perhaps better than Elsa Braun—when they were together in the dining-room they spoke German to each other. When Julie spoke to them they were very polite, and always switched to English, but she had the feeling that they looked on her, for some reason, with some resentment.

'And why would they not?' Rob said to her reasonably, one night after dinner, when they were having coffee together after the German girls had gone, and she had, a little hesitantly, mentioned this to him. 'Look at it from their point of view, Julie. You're younger than they are, and you're prettier. No, you don't need to blush, it's not a compliment I'm after paying you, that is just a fact. You're more senior and, what's perhaps the most difficult thing of all for them, you are on very easy terms with both the doctors.'

Julie, still conscious of her warm cheeks, couldn't help laughing at this. 'Does that really bother them?' she asked, disbelieving.

'It does and all,' Rob assured her. 'They do call both David and me by our Christian names, but it hasn't come easy to them, and here you sail in, and it's all too obvious that you and David know each other, and that you and I get on well together.'

'I suppose that's all true,' she said doubtfully. 'But I hope they won't go on holding that against me!'

Rob refilled their coffee-cups. 'Well, now, girl dear, until they do, you will have to be making do with me for a soulmate,' he told her.

'I suppose I will,' she agreed, smiling.

'Are you likely to be quiet tomorrow, do you think?' he asked her then. 'If you are, I would like to get Meg Winter down to see you.'

'Should be quiet,' Juliè told him, 'unless we have unexpected patients, and we have no clinic—mid-morning would be a good time.'

'I'll take a walk up the hill now to the mission,' said Rob, 'and tell Meg that.' He looked down at her. 'Are you coming with me?'

'No, I—I have some ironing to do,' Julie said quickly and untruthfully, remembering the last time she had walked up the hill with the Irishman.

'The fresh air would do you good,' he said, but Julie shook her head, refusing to respond to the warm teasing in his voice. Another walk in the moonlight with this man, and the possible outcome, seemed all at once a complication she could do without right now.

'Ah, well, perhaps another time,' Rob murmured philosophically as he left her at the door.

Perhaps, Julie thought, as she went into her room. And again, perhaps not, Dr Kennedy.

But if David hadn't been here, bringing back memories of how she had felt about him all those years ago, would she have responded differently, she couldn't help wondering, to Rob Kennedy's light-hearted and easygoing manner?

It was a disturbing thought, and one that she knew it was better not to dwell on.

She was glad that no unexpected patients turned up the next morning, and that she was clear of the routine ward work, by the time Patience told her that Dr Kennedy was coming with the mission lady.

'The clinic's empty, I'll do her check-up there,' she told the girl. 'When you've made tea for the patients, will you bring some for Mrs Winter and me? Thanks, Patience.'

She went to the door to meet Rob and her new patient. As always, the day was hot even at this time, and she was sorry for this woman, who was in advanced pregnancy and still with a few weeks to go. But Meg Winter's face was serene and happy as Rob brought her in.

'I thought you'd have little Faith with you,' said Julie, after Rob had introduced them.

'Sister Nguli has claimed her, and at the moment she's being taken round the general ward, like a film star. She'll bring her over soon.' Meg glanced at Rob, and smiled. 'I don't think David is too impressed.'

'Nonsense, David loves Faith as much as we all do,' Rob told her.

Meg Winter raised her eyebrows. 'In the middle of his ward round?'

Rob shrugged. 'Even David knows things are different here at Tabanduli,' he said.

Even David? Did he mean that David found it less easy to adapt to the less formal way of working here? And did he think that was wrong?

Determinedly, Julie put all thoughts of David out of her mind and took out Meg Winter's folder.

'I'll leave you girls to this,' Rob said then. At the door, he turned. 'Meg, don't you dare walk up the hill, someone will take you up. Walking down was bad enough in this heat.'

When he had gone, Julie looked up from the folder.

'You've had a few frights along the way with this one, Mrs Winter, haven't you?' she said with sympathy.

'Please call me Meg, and can I call you Julie? I've heard so much about you from Rob,' the older woman said. There was a momentary shadow in her blue eyes. 'Yes, I had a threatened miscarriage at five weeks, and again at ten—but thanks to Rob, and a lot of people praying for us, the baby decided to stay put. And surely now everything is all right? I did panic last week, because I thought he wasn't moving, but Rob said I'd just been doing too much.' She put one hand on her swollen stomach, protectively. 'And he's certainly active enough again now!'

Julie helped her on to the bed, and got her foetal stethoscope to check the baby's heartbeat.

'Good and strong and regular,' she said. 'You say he, Meg—did they tell you when you had a scan?'

Meg Winter shook her head. 'No, they said they could, but Steve and I didn't want to know. I just say "he" because it's easier, and because I have a feeling it's a boy. But it won't matter at all, Julie, in fact it would be lovely for Faith to have a sister.'

She lay still while Julie checked her blood-pressure.

'Rob will have told you that we adopted Faith, and that somehow did the trick?'

'Yes, he did—it's incredible how often that happens,' Julie replied, and she made a note of the blood-pressure in Meg's folder. 'Now I just want to check the height of your uterus, and how your baby's lying.'

'Your hands are very strong, but they're gentle,' said Meg, and the unexpected compliment brought a flush of pleasure to Julie's cheeks.

'Everything's fine,' she told her patient when she had completed the check-up. 'I gather you're going to Umtata to have the baby? I'd like to see you again in a week, because as soon as the head is engaged you should be within reach of the hospital.'

'Umtata is all right,' said Meg, and Julie helped her as she got awkwardly off the bed, and dressed. 'I have people I can stay with, and I can take Faith. It wouldn't have been possible if I'd gone to Cape Town or Durban, and Rob says there's no need to worry.'

'I would agree,' Julie told her, 'it looks as if you're all set for a normal birth, and your baby is already a decent size. Oh, here's Patience with tea for us.'

'Tea, and my daughter,' Meg said proudly as Patience came in, with a tiny girl walking not too steadily beside her.

'Oh!' Julie exclaimed, surprised, for she hadn't realised that little Faith was black.

Unfazed, Meg laughed. 'Rob didn't tell you?' she said. 'It probably didn't occur to him.' She lifted the little girl up and held her close. 'Did you see Sister Nguli and all your other friends?' she asked, and the child nodded, and said something.

'She says she had fruit juice, and a biscuit,' Meg translated, and put the child down again.

'Can I take her to speak to the ladies in the ward, Mrs Winter?' Patience asked, and when Meg nodded she held out her hand to the little girl.

'She's adorable,' Julie said, meaning it. 'And she's so friendly. Does she give that big sunny smile to everyone?'

'The whole world is her friend,' Meg said. 'You know, living at the mission, she's always been used to people coming and going.'

Julie poured tea for them both. 'Do you think you'll have any problems, with one child being black and the other white?' she asked.

Meg shook her head, and for a moment Julie glimpsed the determination behind the older woman's serenity.

'No, I don't,' she replied. 'Nor from Faith being adopted, and this one not. There will be complete acceptance right from the start.' She smiled. 'We're not the first couple from the mission to adopt a black child,' she said. 'Soon after we came, the Martins added little Peter to their family—Jean used to say that her biggest problem was that their John, who was much the same age, complained bitterly because he looked dirty much sooner than Peter did! And I guess we can handle problems like that.'

When they had finished having tea, and Julie put the cups back on the tray, Meg stood up.

'Come up and see us some time,' she suggested. 'We usually sit and talk in the living-room in the evenings— come to the service if you want to, but if you don't, come up around nine, have a cup of coffee. I'd like you to meet Steve.'

'I'd like that,' Julie said, and meant it, for she felt the beginning of a bond of friendship with this woman. Meg was different from any of her other friends. She was older, of course, for Julie's closest friends were her own nursing set, and because she had remained in nursing, because she had always loved her work, she had never made any real friend outside nursing.

'Have you any new babies at the moment?' asked Meg.

'Only one,' Julie told her. 'The other two we had went home yesterday.'

'I've been practising on Helen's little Mark,' Meg told her. 'It's going to be fun having two babies around the same age at the mission. We were all worried about this diabetes, but Helen says everything is fine now.'

'Yes, it is,' Julie agreed. 'And next time we'll watch her very carefully.'

She took Meg through to the ward, and listened with admiration and some awe as Meg spoke to the young black woman in her own language, then lifted the two-day-old baby in her arms.

'Even Mark at two weeks seems big compared with this one,' she said softly. 'And Faith seems quite a big girl!' Above the baby's head, her eyes met Julie's. 'I want my baby so much, Julie,' she said, not quite steadily. 'I want him to be safely born.'

'He will be, Meg,' Julie replied, and knew her own voice was unsteady. 'Your baby will be fine.'

When Meg, with Faith's small hand in hers, had gone, Julie went back to complete her folder. She was still writing when the door opened, and the shadow of a tall figure fell on the desk. She looked up, expecting Rob. But it was David.

'I came to see how Meg Winter's check-up went,' he said, and his voice was carefully professional. 'Is everything all right? Head engaged yet?'

Julie told him that the head wasn't yet engaged, and she showed him Meg's folder. He read it swiftly, and handed it back to her.

'As soon as the head is engaged, she must go to Umtata,' he said, and frowned. 'I wish I could persuade her to go to Cape Town instead.'

'She looks all set for a normal birth,' Julie told him, as she had told Meg. 'I don't think there's any need to worry, David—she's fine, the baby's fine, but I do agree that she should go to the big hospital, or be within access to it, as soon as the head engages. I've asked her to come back next week, so we'll see how——'

'Julie,' David said quietly, 'I get the feeling you've been avoiding me.'

Warm colour flooded her cheeks. 'Not really,' she said quickly, untruthfully. 'You've been busy, I've been busy settling in. . .'

Her voice trailed off as his grey eyes held hers.

'Do you remember when we used to go over to the beach at Camps Bay, when we managed to get a day off at the same time, and we liked to go early in the morning, when we could have the beach to ourselves?' he said, and his voice was warm.

Julie turned away. 'I don't really want to remember, David,' she replied evenly.

But even as she said it, she wondered if she was really being honest—with him, and with herself.

CHAPTER FIVE

'SORRY. Am I interrupting?' Rob said from the door.

His voice was cool, and he didn't sound in the least sorry, Julie thought.

'Of course not,' David replied brusquely. 'As you probably guessed, I wanted to know about Meg's check-up, and I wanted Julie's opinion about whether she wouldn't be better to go to Cape Town.'

There was an indefinable change on the Irish doctor's lean brown face, as he looked from David to Julie.

It was true, of course, what David had said, and the last thing Julie wanted was for Rob to think she was disregarding what he had said to her about David's and Sarah's marriage. So she should have been grateful to David for deflecting any possible awkwardness.

And I am, she told herself hastily. Only there was something that made her vaguely uneasy about David's immediate reaction.

'And what do you think Meg should do, Julie?' Rob asked.

Julie held out Meg Winter's folder to him. 'I think there's no reason to worry about her pregnancy now,' she said clearly. 'Everything is proceeding normally, and as soon as the head is engaged she'll go to Umtata.'

Unexpectedly, Rob smiled. 'Just as well you've given her your official blessing on that,' he commented. 'As you'll find out, Meg is the sweetest person—but she can also be one very stubborn lady!' He turned to David. 'I looked over to say that I'm just going to run Faith and Meg up the hill—I'll only be twenty minutes, and everything's quiet on the ward, but I might be five minutes late for the clinic.'

'That's all right, I'll be there,' David replied. 'I'll get back over to the ward now, though.'

The two men walked across the courtyard together, and Julie, after a moment, put Meg Winter's folder away in the filing cabinet and went back through to her ward.

'Well, Mrs Ramphele,' she said cheerfully to the young woman in the end bed in the small labour ward, 'are you going to have your baby before Patience and I go off duty, or are you going to interrupt our supper?'

Because this was such a small hospital, and because it was a mission hospital, and run on necessarily less formal lines, already Julie had found that although her day was supposed to finish at seven, and she was supposed to have two full days and one half day off in the week, if there was a delivery through the night, or on her day off, she was called. She didn't mind this at all. The years of working in the obstetric units in the townships had given her confidence in her own ability, and she knew that no one else on the nursing staff was as competent as she was.

And so it was a question of calling either of the doctors, or Julie, and she was glad to save both David and Rob some work. And also she had to admit that already she had quite a strongly possessive feeling about her ward.

Fortunately the young woman had a quick and normal delivery just before six, and when Monika Jansen came to take over Julie was able to tell her that she was set for a quiet night.

'I do not worry, Sister Norton, for I am able to cope,' Monika Jansen replied coolly.

'I know that, Monika,' Julie returned, determined to keep trying to be less formal. 'But it does make it easier when you don't have to get me over for the delivery, doesn't it?'

I shouldn't have said that, she thought as she went off duty. It was all too obvious that the German girl resented Julie's greater qualifications, and usually Julie was very careful to be as tactful as possible. But it was foolish not to face facts, she told herself, and she certainly wasn't going to fall over backwards to try to get the German nurse to accept her.

The younger one, Elsa, would have been more inclined to be friendly, she thought, but she took her lead from Monika Jansen, and although she was quite prepared to respond a little shyly to Julie when they happened to be in the dining-room together, when Monika was there she would talk only in German to her friend.

When the two German nurses were off duty together in the evening, they usually went off up the hill to join in a church service at the mission. Julie found herself reluctant to accept Meg's invitation on a night when they were there, so she waited until she knew that Monika was working and Elsa was in her room before she went off to walk up to the mission. Rob hadn't returned from the clinic he had gone to, and David had had supper early and gone back to the ward.

It was a hot, still night, with no breath of wind, but Rob had been right, there was a touch of coolness near the top of the hill. I must come up here in daylight, Julie thought, looking around as she reached the cluster of buildings that made up the mission. The view must be magnificent.

Now that she had come she was a little hesitant, but the man who opened the door greeted her warmly.

'Julie, I'm so glad you came,' he said, taking her inside to the big, well-lit room. 'Meg said she hoped you would. I'm Steve Winter. Now, come and meet the others.'

Meg Winter was sitting in a comfortable chair, with her feet up, and she held out her hand to Julie, her face

lighting up. 'We're just going to have coffee,' she said,
'and we're quieter than usual. Helen has gone to feed the
baby, and Brian is with her.' She smiled up at her
husband. 'Are you going to make the coffee, love?'

'Now that you put it like that, I think I am,' Steve
Winter said, and he smiled too. 'While I do, why don't
you take Julie over to see the weaving the women are
doing?'

At the far end of the room, a small group of black
women were working on looms, talking and laughing as
they worked. Meg took Julie across to them, and introduced her.

'Anyone thinking about having a baby will be meeting
Sister Norton,' she told them.

One of the women said something in her own language,
and they all laughed.

'What did she say?' Julie asked.

Meg laughed too. 'She said sometimes the babies come
even without thinking about them!' She touched one of
the brightly woven rugs. 'Isn't this lovely? And they only
learned to weave a few years ago, when one of the big
firms in Cape Town gave us these looms.'

Julie touched the soft clear jewel-like colours of the
weaving. 'This is just what I need to brighten up my
room,' she said with pleasure. 'Could I buy two, maybe?
And then perhaps later one to hang up on the wall?'

'That would be wonderful for all of us,' Meg said.
'Don't decide yet—come and have coffee. If they stop
they'll leave the rugs, and you can choose which you
want. Here's Steve with the coffee.'

They went back to join the big fair-haired man at the
other side of the room, Meg explaining to Julie that the
women would only have coffee when they had finished
work for the evening.

'They don't usually work so late, but tomorrow they'll

be working in the fields, and they wanted to have some more rugs ready to sell.'

It was only when the clock over the fireplace struck ten that Julie realised how quickly the time had passed. Both Steve and Meg were easy to talk to, and she had missed people like this. She was glad that Meg's pregnancy had brought them into contact now.

She chose the two rugs she wanted, and Steve said he would send them down in the morning. As she was leaving, Meg took her into Faith's room. The little girl was asleep on her tummy, with her well-padded little bottom in the air. Her cheek rested on one chubby little hand.

'She really is a pet,' Julie whispered.

'We're so lucky to have her,' Meg murmured, and drew the light cover up over the little girl.

And she's lucky to have you and Steve, Julie thought.

She refused Steve's offer to walk down the hill with her, pointing out that it was clear moonlight and you could see the hospital all the way. The air was cooler now, and she enjoyed the walk down. I'll do this again soon, she promised herself.

The next day was clinic, and when Julie went through into the clinic room she found nine or ten African women waiting for her, talking among themselves, and looking at her with great interest when she went in. There had been six babies born since the previous antenatal clinic, so there were new patients now, some of them, she was very pleased to find, here in the early stages—something that didn't happen often enough. Distance, Rob had told her, was one of the problems, and often women wouldn't commit themselves to a monthly visit to the mission hospital until they were at least six months pregnant.

Julie did the routine check-ups, taking the chance to complete more detailed medical histories on the new patients than had been done before. It was, she had to admit, more than a little frustrating when she was trying to record obstetric history to encounter a blank look, and an admission that the mother didn't remember many details about previous births. Since most of these hadn't taken place here at the hospital, she had to establish what she could by examination, and hope that she might find out more of the actual history as the pregnancy progressed.

But with young Patience and Elsa Braun helping her she got through the folders quickly, and now that she had the women together she decided to start the talks on health education that she planned on giving in her clinics.

Patience made tea, and she and Elsa handed out tea and biscuits, then Julie looked at the half-circle of faces.

'I know you all want to do the best you can for your babies,' she said slowly, reminding herself that these women living in this rural community were considerably less sophisticated than the women in the townships near Cape Town. 'You want to have healthy babies, and you want them to grow into healthy children. Some of the tests we've done here today will show us if you have anything wrong with you, if there is anything we have to pay special attention to. That takes time, and I can only tell you when you come here next—and remember, it's important that you come every time, because we must know how your baby is growing, we must check your blood-pressure, we must find out if your body needs more iron.

'While you are carrying your baby, if you hear of anyone who has measles, or anyone who has TB, don't go near them. For your own sake, and even more, for your baby's sake.'

One of the women murmured something to her neighbour, and Julie stopped, waiting for Patience to translate.

'Mrs Mthembu says her sister is ill with the coughing sickness,' the young African girl said quietly.

'Then tell her she must keep away from her sister until the doctors have made her well,' said Julie. She remembered, then, what Rob Kennedy had said about the *sangomas*, the witch-doctors, treating TB with enemas and emetics. 'And Patience, tell her that her sister must go on seeing the doctors here, and she must go on taking the medicine they give her.'

She told the women then about the importance of body-building foods—knowing as she did so that she was being idealistic, here in this poor rural community—and about the dangers of smoking and drugs of any kind.

'If you need to take any medicine, I will give it to you, or the doctor will give it to you,' she said sternly.

'Quite right, Sister,' Rob agreed, from the open door. He looked around at the women. 'You remember what Sister Norton has been telling you, now. Does everyone understand, or do you want Patience to tell you in your own tongue?'

Everyone nodded, and as they went out they were talking in small groups, all, Julie saw, very earnest.

'Do you think I got through to them?' she asked Rob.

'I don't know, Julie,' he said after a moment, honestly. 'Some of what you told them isn't relevant—oh, there are some who get hold of cigarettes, some who will take patent medicines, but mostly their lives are very simple. It's just a case of growing enough food to feed their families, I'm afraid.'

He sat on the table, his long legs, swinging, and took the cup of tea Patience brought to him.

'Ever heard of the Valley Trust?' he asked her.

'Yes—it's in the Valley of a Thousand Hills, near Durban, isn't it?' Julie replied.

'The people who started the Valley Trust had a dream,'

the Irish doctor said quietly. 'A dream of teaching people how to help themselves—teaching them better ways to grow vegetables, teaching them proper nutrition, teaching them to be self-sufficient. And they do that. I spent a couple of months there before I came here, filling in for a friend who works there. One of the things I want to do here—and I have Steve and Meg in on it too—is to raise money to send two or three people to the Valley to learn all they can, and then to come back here, put it into practice and teach other people.'

His blue eyes were far away.

'And we'll do it,' he said, almost to himself. 'We'll do it. It may take time, but we'll do it. They're hard up at the mission, of course, I know that.'

Julie looked at him, for this was a side of the young doctor she hadn't seen before.

He stood up, unembarrassed by her gaze. 'And are we not supposed to be a country of dreamers, back in Ireland?' he asked her, his Irish accent suddenly much more pronounced. 'And do you not think it is a worthwhile dream, girl dear?'

'I do indeed,' Julie agreed warmly. She might, she thought, mention this in her next letter home, and perhaps her father, through the Rotary Club he belonged to, could do something.

'How long were you listening for?' she asked Rob then. 'I didn't know you were there.'

'Long enough,' Rob replied, 'to see that you're doing a good job, and I particularly liked your commercial for the TB treatment! Well, I'd better be getting back, or the big boss will be wondering where I am.'

'I never know if you're serious or not,' said Julie, going to the door with him. 'David isn't really the big boss, surely you're both here on equal terms?'

'Well, he was here a few months before me, so

technically he does have the seniority, but I don't let it
bother me,' Rob said jauntily.

Julie hadn't meant to say it, but she did. 'You don't
really get on too well together, the two of you, do you?'

Afterwards she thought she liked him all the more for
his refusal to be drawn into this.

'Well, perhaps we're just not soulmates, but we work
well enough together,' he said, and with a wave to
Patience and Elsa he was off.

The clinic had been more tiring than Julie had
expected it to be, and she was glad of her day off the next
day, glad that there was no one in the maternity ward
other than two women with babies of one and two days
old, so that she could relax and know there was no
imminent delivery. Luxury, she thought the next morning, to hear people hurrying down the corridor to have
breakfast, and to start work, while she could wait until
the dining-room was deserted, and she could take the
new Wilbur Smith over, and sit and read over her coffee
and toast.

And after that the day stretched ahead of her. It wasn't
quite so hot, and she thought she might follow the road
that led further down into the valley, where there was
surely a river, judging by the line of trees and bushes.
She put on trousers and a shirt, and took a hat with her
for the walk back.

She was right about the river, she found, although she
thought her Scottish grandmother would probably say it
was 'just a burn'. But river or burn, it was pleasant to see
the water flowing over its stony bed, and there was a
fairly well-worn path along the side, so she could follow
it.

Where the trees were at their thickest she found a tiny
waterfall, and a pool at the foot of it. Oh, she thought

longingly, if only I'd brought my swimming-costume with me!

Tentatively she put one foot in the water. It was just as she had thought it would be, delightfully cool with the stones under it and the trees above it. And there was no one around. The nearest village was miles away, the hospital was way up the hill, and the mission station itself even further.

Julie stripped off her clothes, and slid into the water from a large rock at the edge. It was cooler than her foot had indicated, and she gasped, but it was lovely, and in a moment she was well and truly in and swimming over towards the waterfall, where she found she could swim in behind it and look out through a curtain of shining water. She swam back to the rock where she had left her clothes, and now that she knew the pool was deep enough she dived in. Then she swam behind the waterfall again, and lay stretched out on her front, with the spray playing on her body.

Marvellous, she thought, sliding into the water again. I'm so glad I found this place.

She had reached the middle of the pool when she saw him.

Rob, sitting on the rock next to the one where she had left her clothes. He had a towel wrapped round him.

'Hi, Julie, I see you've found our swimming-pool,' he said cheerfully. 'How's the water? I must say I didn't expect company when I grabbed an hour off to come down, but all the nicer. I'll join you.'

He stood up and took his towel off. He was wearing white swimming-shorts, and his body was very brown.

'Wait, Rob—wait a minute,' Julie said, managing to find her voice. 'I—I——'

'You're not going to tell me the water's too cold, surely?' said Rob, and he put one foot in.

Julie gulped, and sank down as far as she could. 'No, the water's fine,' she told him. 'But——'

'Race you to the waterfall,' he challenged, and got into the water.

'I haven't got a swimming-costume on,' she said flatly.

Rob, already close to her, raised his eyebrows. 'You don't say!' he murmured, astonishment in his voice. 'Well, now, that's a problem, isn't it?'

He was close enough for her to see the laughter in the dark blue of his eyes.

'We have two possible solutions,' he said thoughtfully, treading water beside her—and Julie was extremely grateful for the brown of the water. 'I could join you, and we could both skinny-dip, and then you would be feeling less embarrassed, perhaps?'

'No, thank you,' Julie replied firmly. 'I've been swimming long enough, I really just want to get out now.'

'Yes, I thought that would be the other solution,' Rob said, and there was regret in his voice. 'Well, then, I will just have to be a gentleman and turn my back until you are respectable again.'

'Thank you,' she returned, even more firmly.

The Irishman turned away, and gazed so fixedly at the waterfall that Julie couldn't help smiling as she swam over to the rock and pulled herself out.

'Can I use your towel to dry myself, Rob?' she called.

'Of course,' he replied. 'I feel a bit like Sir Walter Raleigh with Queen Elizabeth. And fancy my not noticing that you had no towel lying there with your clothes, for of course if I had I would surely have realised that you hadn't come down here with the thought of swimming.'

Julie, rubbing herself dry and pulling her briefs and bra and her trousers and shirt on, stopped. Of course he must have seen that she had no towel, and of course he must have known that she had no bathing-costume on.

'You can turn round,' she called. And when he was facing her she said sternly, 'And I want to know how long you were there before I saw you, Rob Kennedy!'

His dark blue eyes were wide and innocent as he pushed the wet dark hair back from his forehead.

'Not long at all, girl dear,' he assured her. 'I was just after sitting here peacefully, admiring the scenery, you might say, when to my complete surprise I realised that you were there.' His lips twitched. 'But of course,' he told her earnestly, 'I never for a moment expected that Sister Norton would be skinny-dipping!'

He swung himself out of the water and sat beside her on the rock.

'I've been thinking about what you said, Julie,' he said then.

'What I said?' Julie repeated, taken aback—and, she knew, more than a little disturbed by his closeness to her. 'Here's your towel—you'd better get dried,' she said quickly.

'What you said about chemistry,' he said, and moved closer to her, purposefully. 'It's an interesting thought— a very interesting thought.'

CHAPTER SIX

Rob's lips were warm on Julie's, gentle at first and then not at all gentle. And once again Julie found herself responding to his kiss with everything in her.

'Well, now,' Rob said softly, his lips still close to hers, 'there's a thing now, Julie, this chemistry works just as well by daytime as it does in the moonlight. I was wondering about that, I must say.'

Julie moved back from him, because if she hadn't she knew she would have moved closer. 'I think it's time I was getting back,' she told him.

His blue eyes were very dark, this close, she found herself noticing. Dark, and with a warm, sleepy look that was extremely disturbing.

'You have the whole day off,' he reminded her. 'I know, because I asked Elsa.'

Julie scrambled to her feet. 'And I have no intention of spending any more of it here with you, Rob Kennedy,' she said firmly. 'This is all very pleasant, but it could lead to complications.'

'I like the sound of that, I do indeed,' he murmured, and in spite of herself Julie began to laugh.

And that, she thought later, was perhaps fortunate, for laughter dispelled the distinctly strange and disturbing feelings she had, being this close to Rob, with her lips still warm from his kiss.

But not really so strange, she told herself reasonably. After all, Rob Kennedy was—no, not really good-looking, perhaps, but undoubtedly attractive. It was a good thing that both he and she had spelled out the ground rules right at the start—he knew she wasn't looking for any serious involvement, and she knew he would make the most of what life offered him—wasn't that what he had said, that first day?

They walked back along the river path, and up the hill to the hospital, talking now about the hospital itself, about their work. Julie had seen already that under his light-heartedness Rob was serious about his work, and she liked that.

Neither he nor she mentioned David, and she was glad of that, for it seemed safer and wiser for her to avoid thinking about the man who had meant so much to her all those years ago. If she could.

It was fortunate, she told herself, that most of the time her work and David's work kept them apart. He did occasionally come over to the maternity ward, and if she needed a doctor, and Rob wasn't there, of course she would call him.

But a few days after her day off, it was David who needed her help.

Julie knew that Sister Nguli was in bed with flu that day, and she knew, too, that with Monika Jansen away in Umtata for a few days, this left them short-staffed. And when Rob left to take a clinic in a distant village David was left with only Elsa in the general ward and in casualty.

It was mid-afternoon when Elsa came hurrying across. 'Sister Norton, Dr Shaw needs you, right away,' she said breathlessly. 'He says can you leave Patience in charge here.'

Julie looked around. The three patients were settled for the afternoon, and the only one in labour wasn't likely to need her for a few hours. Swiftly she gave Patience instructions, and followed Elsa across the dusty courtyard.

David was in the small operating theatre which was all they had for any emergencies. He glanced up from the young man on the bed.

'Thanks, Sister. Elsa can't leave the ward, and I need help. Simon here has got a fish-hoek in his hand, and he's been very foolish—instead of coming right away, he's left it two days.'

The young man, his eyes closed, murmured that he had thought it would come out by itself, Doctor.

'This will be very painful,' David said to Julie, his voice low. 'Without Rob here, I can't give him a general, but he's had a pretty good jab of pethidine.'

Without needing any further instructions, Julie put on a gown and gloves, after she had checked the prepared instruments. It was a long time since she had done any theatre work, but her training came to the fore instinctively.

Simon was already drowsy, and she swabbed his hand and draped a sterile towel around it. By the time David had scrubbed up, the young man was asleep.

'Look at this,' said David, and pointed to a thin red line running up Simon's arm. 'The infection's spread to the lymphatic system—we'll keep him in for a couple of days, have him on antibiotics.'

Years ago, when they had worked together at Groote Schuur, Julie had seen him, a young houseman then, working in the theatre, and suddenly, as she looked at his fair head bent over what he was doing, absorbed, she had the strange feeling that the years between then and now had gone.

'I'll have to extend the entry wound,' David murmured, more to himself than to her. She handed him the scalpel he needed for that, and watched as he extended the wound, and then carefully extracted the fish-hoek.

Silently she passed him a swab, and he began to clean the deepened wound.

'That should do it,' he said at last. 'I'm not stitching completely, I want to leave a drain in—yes, that small one will do—in case there's any more poison.'

Julie bandaged the young man's hand, and then cleaned up what they had used.

'Nice not to have to tell you what to do, Julie,' David said suddenly.

She turned round. He had taken off his white jacket, and he looked younger, more vulnerable, in his vest. Younger, and so very much the David she remembered. The David she had loved.

That was dangerous thinking, and Julie knew it. She took off the overall she had pulled on top of her uniform, and then took off the theatre cap.

'If that's all you need me for, I'd better get back,' she said quickly. 'I've left Patience in charge, and she might need me.'

'Julie,' David said quietly, 'you're always running away from me.'

She couldn't deny this, because it was true.

'Running away from me, and perhaps running away from yourself,' he added. He came over to her, and put both hands on her shoulders, looking down into her face. 'You must have hated me,' he said, his voice low, 'for going back to Sarah.'

'Hated you? No, I—didn't hate you,' Julie replied, with difficulty.

No, she hadn't hated him. Missed him, longed for him, wept for him, but she had respected his loyalty, she had accepted that he felt that Sarah needed him more than she did.

'It wasn't an easy decision to make,' David said now, quietly.

Julie said nothing. Part of her knew that she should stop him now before he said anything more, but another part desperately wanted him to go on, to tell her——

'I always hoped that you knew that,' he said.

'Yes, I did,' she replied. 'I—David, you shouldn't——'

'I know that,' he said. 'But I had to say it.'

She turned away. 'It's too late, David,' she said, not quite steadily.

His hands were on her shoulders. 'Is it?' he asked.

He was very close to her. And suddenly all Julie's professional instincts told her that this was wrong. This was not the time or the place for David to kiss her, for him to say these things. Maybe there never would be a time or a place, maybe it was all better left unsaid. But certainly not here, not now.

'I'm going back to my ward, David,' she said, and now her voice was steady. And without waiting for him to reply, she turned and went out.

There were no further emergencies while the general ward and casualty were under-staffed over the next two days, and she was glad of that.

'It does just show how much we could do with another senior sister,' she remarked to Steve and Meg Winter a few evenings later, when she walked up the hill to the mission station to visit them.

Steve shook his head. 'The mission can't afford any more staff, Julie. Sorry, but I've just had a copy of last year's annual report—we really do work from hand to mouth.'

Meg put her hand over his. 'But something always turns up, doesn't it?' she said.

He covered her hand with his. 'Yes, love, it does—but we have to be realistic. We're mighty lucky to have you folks at the hospital, Julie, we know that.'

Meg shifted awkwardly in her chair, then smiled, as both Julie and Steve looked at her quickly.

'You really are both a couple of fusspots,' she said teasingly. 'I'm uncomfortable, that's all—and this baby is taking its time, the head isn't even engaged yet.'

She looked up as the door opened and Rob came in.

'Rob, how nice to see you,' she said. 'Even if it is late!'

'I know it is,' Rob agreed, 'but I was late getting back, and although I did want to say hello to you two, and to see how you're doing, Meg, I really came up to escort Julie down the hill—the wind's got up, and the clouds are scudding across the sky so much that it's very dark.'

'And you thought Julie might be afraid to walk down in the dark alone?' Meg asked, laughter in her voice.

'I did and all,' Rob replied, unabashed. 'For I knew she would not be letting Steve leave you, to see her home. Thanks, I will join you in a cup of coffee first, though.'

Half an hour later, he told Meg firmly that she should be in bed, and he and Julie said goodnight, and started down the hill. He was right, there was a storm building up, and the wind was fierce.

'I don't want you blown away,' said Rob, and he took her arm in his.

'I'm a little too substantial for that,' Julie told him, laughing, but glad that he was there with her.

When they reached the shelter of the hospital walls, they were both breathless.

'Thanks, Rob, I'm glad you came,' Julie said, meaning it.

He looked down at her. 'So am I, girl dear,' he said softly.

The wind howling so close to them, and the small sheltered corner they were in, made the two of them seem very much alone, Julie found herself thinking. Just as she and David had been alone in the theatre the other day.

She turned her head away, and Rob's lips brushed against her hair.

'I must go in,' she said breathlessly.

His hands were on her shoulders, and suddenly they were still. 'It's because of him that you don't want me to kiss you,' he said.

She couldn't deny that. 'You're—very perceptive,' she replied, with difficulty.

'Where you are concerned, perhaps I am,' he said, and his voice was strained. 'For heaven's sake, Julie, you can't have been carrying a torch for this man for ten years!'

'I haven't!' she returned indignantly. 'I've hardly given him a thought for years.'

And that was true. But coming here, seeing David again, learning that he and his wife were separated—it made things very difficult. And Rob should understand that.

Suddenly she was angry with him. 'It's nothing to do with you, anyway,' she said, knowing she sounded childish.

'I'm not so sure about that,' he replied. 'I don't want anything to come in the way of Sarah and David getting together again, and——' He hesitated.

'And what?' Julie asked, her voice low.

She felt his hands tighten on her shoulders.

'And I don't want to see you hurt,' he said.

She was absurdly touched by this. 'Thank you for that, Rob,' she said shakily. 'But I can look after myself.' She touched his cheek. 'And now I really am going inside,' she told him. The anger she had felt towards him had gone, and she knew that he realised that. For a moment his arm around her shoulder drew her closer, and she thought his lips brushed her hair again.

'Maybe you'd better,' he agreed, and the old light-hearted note was back in his voice. 'And for heaven's sake go past Monika's door softly, because she will undoubtedly think the worst, and that's a terrible waste, is it not, when there is nothing to be thought?'

Julie laughed. 'I suppose it is,' she agreed. 'Goodnight, Rob.'

Rather to her amusement, as she went along the corridor to her own room Monika Jansen did open her door and look out.

'Oh!' she said, with pretended surprise. 'I wondered if something was wrong, someone coming in as late as this.'

Julie, with her door open, turned back and smiled sweetly at the German nurse. 'Nothing's wrong, thank you, Monika, nothing at all. So you can go back to sleep.'

For a moment the hostility in Monika's pale blue eyes disturbed her, but there was nothing she could do about it. Already she and Elsa were on better terms. A few days before, during the clinic, Julie had taken Elsa aside and asked her to go over and see if Dr Kennedy could come to check one of their patients.

'Tell him I'm pretty sure it's a breech presentation,' she said quietly. 'Left sacro-lateral—I don't want to say anything to alarm the mother when he comes, so tell him that.'

Rob, when he came, confirmed Julie's diagnosis, and agreed with her that he would make no attempt now to turn the baby, as this could happen naturally nearer the due date.

'What special danger is there to the baby, Sister— Julie?' Elsa asked, when the clinic was over.

'Intracranial haemorrhage because of rapid compression—hypoxia—this happens sometimes because the cord prolapses, and we have to move fast then,' Julie told her. 'But the optimum time for turning the baby is between the thirty-second and the thirty-sixth week, and that's what Dr Kennedy will wait for.' And seeing the girl's anxious expression, 'But Elsa, I've delivered quite a few breech babies, and although you do have to be aware of the problems you learn the best way to deliver. So don't worry, this baby will be fine, whatever.'

But the real breakthrough with the younger German nurse, Julie often thought later, was a week later. Julie was in the duty-room, writing up the charts for the day, when Elsa came in, white-faced.

'Mrs Myeni, the one who had her baby last night—she is bleeding so badly, and already she is in shock!'

Julie hurried through to the ward. The massive haemorrhage had happened very quickly, and the woman was on the point of collapse.

'Pads,' Julie said. 'Lot of them, and stat. Oh—I mean quickly, Elsa.'

Swiftly, efficiently, she got the bleeding under control, and then she gave an injection of ergometrine intravenously.

'That should act almost immediately,' she told Elsa. 'Help me to set up a drip, and then go for Dr Kennedy, or Dr Shaw if Dr Kennedy isn't there.'

She had, she knew, done all that was necessary, and already the grey pallor of shock had left the woman's face. By the time Rob arrived, striding in with Elsa, the thready pulse-rate had settled, and she was checking the blood-pressure.

'Good, Sister, there's nothing more you need to do,' Rob told her when he had examined the woman. 'We'll keep her in for a couple of days extra, though, and watch her.'

When he had gone, Elsa followed Julie back to the duty-room. 'What causes this, Julie?' she asked.

Elsa had no midwifery qualification, and Julie was more and more certain that this was a necessity here at Tabanduli.

'It can be mismanagement of third stage,' Julie said. 'But it wasn't. She's a grande multipara—this is her fifth baby—so it's most likely that she has a lax uterus. I think we must do all we can to persuade her to come to our family planning clinic.' She looked up at the young woman standing beside her. 'That's something else you've learned, Elsa—you should consider doing midwifery, you know. Specially if you mean to stay on here, or at any other mission hospital.'

Elsa turned away, but not before Julie had seen that she was close to tears. 'I am not a good nurse, Julie—I do not keep calm. I am very frighten when I see how she is bleeding.'

Julie stood up, and put one arm around Elsa's shoulders. 'I was very frightened too, the first haemorrhage I saw,' she told her. 'But now you know how to deal with it—next time, grab some pads right away, even before you get me. No, Elsa, you're doing fine.'

After that, any time they were in the dining-room together Elsa would stop speaking German, and include Julie in the conversation—in spite of Monika's all too clear disapproval.

It was in the dining-room a few nights later, when Elsa and Monika had left to go to a church service at the mission, taking Patience with them, leaving Julie having coffee with Rob and David, that Rob turned to David.

'You'll be expecting the children here for the holidays, David?' he asked.

Julie could see that David was taken aback, perhaps

not as much by the question itself as by the direct way Rob had asked it.

'Yes—yes, I am,' he replied.

'You will be looking forward to that, I'm sure,' Rob said pleasantly. He turned to Julie. 'We all enjoy having Timothy and Clare here—you'll like them, they're nice kids.' He turned back to David. 'And is Sarah coming this time?' he asked conversationally.

David stood up, and his chair scraped harshly on the floor. 'No, she isn't,' he said brusquely, and turned and went out of the room.

Julie looked at Rob. 'Did you have to do that?' she asked him.

For once there was no warmth in Rob's dark blue eyes. 'Yes, I did,' he replied. 'I knew they were coming, and I thought it was time you knew too!'

Julie lifted her chin. 'Well, then,' she said, knowing she sounded defiant, 'so now I know. It isn't really any big deal, Rob—obviously David's children would be coming to visit him some time, he—he just doesn't happen to have mentioned it to me, that's all.'

'No, he hasn't,' Rob agreed, and his voice was tight. 'And until you see him as Clare and Timothy's father, and as Sarah's husband, you're going to go on thinking of him as your lost love, Julie.'

This was too close to home, and Julie felt a warm, defensive colour flood her cheeks. 'That's nonsense,' she said quickly—too quickly, she knew. 'And I've said it before, Rob, but really it's nothing to do with you. We're all old enough to look after ourselves.'

'I'm not so sure about that,' Rob returned. 'And I reckon these kids need someone looking out for their interests, if nothing else. And——' he hesitated, but only for a moment, and now his eyes were very dark. 'And I don't think it is a good thing for them, Julie, that you and their father are getting all sentimental about something that happened ten years ago.' He came over to her and put his hands on her shoulders, and now his voice was soft. 'Don't be shutting me out with that look, girl dear—be honest with yourself.'

Julie turned away. 'You don't understand how it was, Rob,' she said shakily. 'You don't know how we felt, David and I.'

'Tell me, then.' He looked around at the stark and basic dining-room, and shook his head. 'Not here,' he said flatly. 'Come outside.'

It was hot and still, and there was a distant rumble of thunder. And in spite of the heat Julie shivered as they walked slowly up the road that led to the mission buildings at the top of the hill.

She was grateful, she realised, for this chance to make Rob understand, to let him see David in a better light than he obviously did. David, and perhaps herself as well. For it surprised her to realise just how much his opinion mattered to her.

'We were working together in theatre,' she said steadily. 'David was a houseman, and I was a second-year student nurse. We—became friendly.'

For a moment she was silent, knowing how inadequate these words were. Remembering their eyes meeting, above theatre masks. Remembering a moment of breathlessness when they had met as they both left the theatre. Remembering so much.

'I didn't know, at the start, that he was engaged,' she said with difficulty. And then, with honesty, 'But I don't know if it would have made any difference, Rob. David told me quite soon all about Sarah. They'd known each other for ages, you see, and both their families expected them to get engaged—her father was medical superintendent of the hospital where David usually worked during the holidays——'

She was conscious of Rob's silence, of the stiffness of his body beside her in the warm darkness.

'I'm sure they were very fond of each other,' she said quickly. 'But it was different, the way David and I felt about each other. They'd been so young, you see, they just didn't know.'

'Oh, Julie, my dear,' said Rob, and the unexpected gentleness of his voice made her heart turn over, 'you were not that old yourself, you know—eighteen, was it?'

'Nearly nineteen,' Julie told him defensively. 'And nursing makes you grow up pretty fast, Rob, you must know that.'

The memories crowded back now. She had not been happy, thinking about the girl he was engaged to, but they had loved each other, she and David, surely this Sarah would understand that.

'Did he tell you he was going to break his engagement to Sarah?' Rob asked then.

Julie hesitated. This was something she had thought about often, in those early months after she and David had parted.

'No,' she said at last, honestly. 'No, he didn't actually say that. But, knowing how we felt about each other, I thought he was just waiting for the right time to tell Sarah.'

'To tell her what?' Rob asked.

'To tell her that they'd made a mistake, that they'd been too young. To tell her that he loved me,' she returned, her voice clear and cool.

Above them there was a flash of lightning, and she moved closer to him, instinctively. He put one arm around her, and once again his voice was gentle.

'But he didn't tell her that?' he asked.

Julie shook her head. 'Sarah had been ill,' she said quietly. 'I don't know what it was, but—David couldn't do it. He said—he hadn't realised how much she needed him, and he——'

'I couldn't live with myself, Julie, if I walked out on her,' he had said, and his grey eyes had been shadowed with unhappiness.

She didn't tell Rob that. That was too private, too personal.

'He said he was going back home, and he was going to marry Sarah,' she said, her voice even. And then, because Rob said nothing in reply, she looked up at him in the warm darkness. 'He was loyal, you see, he couldn't let her down. I always admired that in him, a man who wouldn't let a girl down when she needed him, when she was ill.'

'So that's how you see it,' said Rob, and she realised, with wonder, that there was pity in his voice. 'Oh, Julie girl, you were indeed very young!'

She pulled away from his arm. 'I was old enough,' she told him coolly. And then, because she didn't want him to have the wrong idea, she said quickly, 'Look, Rob, I was pretty heartbroken at first, I admit that. But I certainly haven't been sitting around for ten years thinking about David Shaw.'

And that was true. She'd had fun, plenty of fun, and she'd gone out with quite a few men. All right, she hadn't had any serious relationships with anyone in these years, but that was just how it had happened.

Once again she shivered. 'Does this thunder mean anything?' she asked him, and hoped he would accept that she didn't want to talk any more about herself and David all those years ago.

'Difficult to tell,' he replied, as they began walking back down the hill towards the hospital. 'Sometimes this build-up goes on, and nothing happens. Apparently a couple of years ago, though, the rains came so early and so heavily that the river was flooded and the bridge was down. Last year wasn't bad, though. In any case, rain isn't likely to be bothering a fellow like me, born and brought up in Ireland. Sure and it's the lack of it that's more of a problem.'

He looked down at her. 'My uncle Pat emigrated to Australia,' he told her, and although it was dark she knew by his voice that he was smiling, that the somewhat formidable and unexpectedly serious Dr Kennedy had gone, and this was the familiar Rob again. 'He did very well, got himself a job on a sheep farm, married the owner's daughter, and inherited the sheep farm, and it a great piece of land, half as big as Ireland, according to Uncle Pat. Well, now, there he was set for life, and a Rolls-Royce so that the sheep would not be licking his neck when he drove from the one end of the property to the other, and suddenly he got so homesick for Ireland, and rain, that he persuaded his wife to sell up, and back they came and went into pigs instead of sheep, and he's as happy as Larry, and the more it rains the happier he is.'

'And what about his wife?' asked Julie, smiling too. 'Doesn't she mind the rain?'

'I think she minds the pigs more than she minds the rain, them being less sweet to the nose than the sheep, and closer at hand too, as you might say,' Rob said.

'You are a ridiculous man,' Julie told him. 'I don't believe you have an Uncle Pat at all!'

'What a terrible thing, to have such a distrustful nature, and me as honest as the day is long,' Rob told her.

They had reached the corner of the hospital building, and he stopped.

'Off you go now,' he told her, 'and have a good night's

sleep.' But his hand on her arm stopped her. 'Goodnight, Julie,' he said.

His lips brushed hers, and his arms held her close to him for a moment, then he let her go.

'Away with you, woman,' he told her, 'before you have me forgetting all my good resolutions!' And without giving her a chance to reply he left her, turning at his own door to raise a hand in farewell.

Julie went along the corridor to her room. Just for a moment she couldn't help wondering what he would have done if she had allowed herself to respond to that brief kiss.

Allowed?

The word in her thoughts brought her up short, with the tacit admission that she had wanted his kiss to go on longer.

She sat down on her bed, bewildered, confused. She had gone out with him with all her thoughts of David, of the memories of the time they had been in love with each other. And talking to Rob about it had made it all even more real. And yet here she sat now, wishing that Rob had kissed her properly!

Chemistry, she reminded herself. Just chemistry.

What was that old song, one of Mum's favourites? 'Your lips are much too close to mine, beware, my foolish heart.'

And that's just what you have, Julie Norton, she told herself severely. A very foolish heart!

The small maternity ward always had a few patients, and although Julie and Patience, and sometimes Elsa, were never worked off their feet, there was always something happening.

'And it's a funny thing,' Julie said to Elsa one afternoon when they were having a quick cup of tea in the duty-room, 'how one delivery seems to get everyone else going! Look at us yesterday—three patients, all of them looking as if it would be hours before they delivered, then one has her baby, and within an hour the other two babies are born too—just as well they were all normal deliveries.'

There was a knock at the door, and they both looked up. Sister Nguli stood there.

'I came over quickly in my tea-break,' she said, 'to tell you that the message has come that my niece is coming in, her membranes have ruptured—Nurse Jansen will stand in in my ward so that I can come over right away.'

Julie stood up. This was something that had been worrying her, and she had hoped that it might work out that Sister Nguli's niece came in to have her baby while her aunt was unable to leave her ward.

'Sister Nguli, are you quite sure you want to do this?' she asked, carefully. 'I know the idea is nice, you delivering your niece's baby, but sometimes when it's someone close to you it's difficult to keep your professional detachment.'

The big woman shook her head. 'Do not worry, Sister Norton, everything will be fine—you know yourself that Thandi has been so well through her pregnancy it will be an easy birth, and I will catch the baby, and the next day Thandi will go home.' She smiled. 'I know I have less experience than you do, Sister Norton, but I have delivered many babies, all the same.'

'I know that,' Julie replied, after a moment. 'But not your own niece's, Sister Nguli.'

Sister Nguli smiled again. 'Everything will go well,' she said. 'I will go back just now, and you can tell me when Thandi comes in.'

There was nothing more Julie could do. Sister Nguli was right, there was no reason why young Thandi shouldn't have her baby easily, with her aunt there with her. And yet——

I'm worrying too much, Julie told herself, I'll just have to keep an eye on how things go.

And certainly, at first, there seemed to be no problem. The young woman was only in the first stage of labour, with dilation of the cervix proceeding steadily. Thandi seemed pleased to have her aunt with her, and since there was no other patient in labour they had the small ward to themselves.

'I'm here if you do need me,' Julie said, and she went back to the duty-room.

The routine work of the ward kept both Elsa Braun and her occupied, and, since one of the babies born the day before had to be bottle-fed, that took up time too. So it was with some surprise that Julie realised that nothing seemed to be happening in the labour ward.

She went to the door. 'Everything all right?' she asked cheerfully.

'Oh, yes,' Sister Nguli replied. 'You know how it is with first babies, they take their time.'

Julie hesitated. But the girl in the bed looked reasonably comfortable, and Sister Nguli was, after all, a qualified midwife too. There wasn't really any reason for Julie to suggest that she should check the patient's condition, and the foetal heartbeat.

Often, in her years as a midwife, Julie had come to accept, though, that there were times when you had to follow your intuition, your instinctive feeling that something was wrong. She had that feeling now, and when another hour had passed she knew she couldn't ignore it any longer.

She went into the labour ward, and over to Sister Nguli. 'Can I have a word with you, Sister Nguli?' she said quietly. She smiled at the young woman on the bed.

'It's all right, Thandi, we're right here at the door, we're not leaving you.'

This was difficult. Sister Nguli was older than she was, and her position was more senior. But she had less experience in midwifery, Julie reminded herself, and there was the added complication of the family relationship.

'Sister Nguli,' she said, her voice low, 'surely Thandi has been in second stage too long now?'

'It is long, Sister Norton,' the older woman agreed quickly, defensively, 'but as you see I have set up an oxytocin drip, and IV fluid.'

Julie hesitated. 'Would you mind if I checked her too?' she asked carefully.

For a moment the nurse's dark eyes held hers. Julie kept her own eyes steady, and then, to her relief, Sister Nguli nodded.

'I think perhaps it would be a good idea,' she replied.

Julie went over to the young woman in the bed. Swiftly, professionally, she checked the dilation of the cervix, the mother's blood-pressure, and then the foetal heartbeat. The result made her glance unobtrusively at the chart, before she rechecked.

Always, when she had to do this, she remembered her old obstetrics lecturer saying, 'Whatever you do in the labour ward, don't do or say anything that might panic the patient. Sure, she has to know if something is wrong, but she has to be told calmly. So—foetal distress, now— maybe you've made a mistake, so recheck that heartbeat.'

But her second check confirmed the first. The heart-beat had slowed down, it was below a hundred and twenty beats a minute.

She looked at Sister Nguli. 'A hundred and twenty, I make it,' she said, her voice matter-of-fact.

'What do you think we should do, Sister Norton?' the

African sister asked, and there was no resentment in her voice. Perhaps, Julie thought, relief.

Julie already knew what had to be done. 'We'll stop the oxytocin drip, but leave the IV fluid,' she said. 'Elsa will go and get Dr Kennedy. Meanwhile, Thandi, let me help you to lie on your side—that's better, I'm sure, more comfortable for you. This whole business is taking too long, Thandi, your baby is getting tired. Dr Kennedy will——'

'No, I do not want my baby cut out!' the girl protested, obviously frightened. 'Aunt Agnes, you said I would not need to be cut!'

Julie put her hand over the girl's. 'Thandi,' she said firmly, 'this has to be done. Your baby is a little tired now, but if Dr Kennedy delivers it soon it will be fine. If we wait, the baby will get more tired.'

'Aunt Agnes?' the girl said, turning to Sister Nguli.

'Sister Norton is right, Thandi,' the African sister said, firmly too. 'This has to be done, for your baby's safety. Dr Kennedy has cut to bring many babies safely into the world.'

Julie knew, from talking to Rob, that if it was possible any patients needing delivery by Caesarean section were taken to the big hospital in Umtata. But there were always the cases, he had said, where there was no time, where an emergency Caesar had to be done here, and they were prepared for that here in the small labour ward, instead of having to use the theatre over in the general hospital, for here they had everything for the mother and for the baby.

The foetal heartbeat had dropped further—it was almost a hundred now. Julie hoped she had succeeded in keeping her concern from the girl on the bed, but when the door opened and Rob came in, his white coat flying, her eyes met Sister Nguli's in shared relief.

Swiftly, competently, Rob examined the young woman, talking easily to her, and Julie could see Thandi relax.

'Right, Thandi, first an injection to make you sleepy,' he said, and before the girl could look alarmed he had given her an injection.

Julie knew how incredibly quick a Caesarean section had to be, but working out in the townships, where their patients were always taken into hospital by Flying Squad, it was a long time since she had seen one done. His voice low and crisp, Rob gave her instructions. David was out at a clinic, so Julie would have to supervise the anaesthetic.

'But it's all right,' Rob said reassuringly, 'I'm used to keeping an eye on that too, and it's a light anaesthetic, she'll be out of it soon.'

He was ready to operate now. For a moment, above their masks, his dark blue eyes met Julie's.

'We'll do fine, all of us,' he said softly.

From the first incision to the moment when the uterus was exposed and the baby taken out, and handed to Sister Nguli, it was unbelievably quick. Rob's hands moved swiftly, efficiently, doing the first deep stitches to close the wound, and then the neat stitching of the final layer.

'How's the baby?' he asked then, turning round.

'He's fine,' said Sister Nguli, relief in her voice. 'Colour good, breathing normal, and he doesn't seem distressed.'

'We got him out in good time,' Rob said to Julie. He turned to Sister Nguli. 'You know what to do, Sister—suction, aspirate, keep him warm—that was a good yell he gave, so I don't think he'll be any problem, but I'll be back to have a look at him in an hour or so. And Sister Norton, keep the mother on her side, with a pillow behind her shoulders, and an IV drip of glucose. Pulse every fifteen minutes for three hours, and of course watch for any sign of haemorrhage. And blood-pressure now, and then every two hours.'

He threw his theatre gown and his mask down.

'You're going to be busy,' he told her cheerfully. 'Keep me in touch.'

We certainly are going to be busy, Julie thought, looking around at the labour ward that would have to be cleaned and got ready for the next lady in waiting, thinking of all the medical checks to be done for both Thandi and her baby.

But none of that mattered. The only really important thing was that the baby was safely delivered, and the mother was fine.

'Sister Norton,' Sister Nguli said, beside her, 'I know we are going to be busy, and there will not be much time, but I have to say this now.' Her arms tightened around the baby in her arms. 'You were right,' she said, her eyes on Julie's face. 'Because I am close to Thandi, I did not have the detachment I should have. If she had been another patient, I would have known that a Caesarean section had to be done. I—want to thank you for that.'

It had not been easy for her to say that, Julie could see. 'I'm just so glad Thandi and the baby are all right, Sister Nguli,' she said, not quite steadily. 'Now, we'd better get these two sorted out, and then clean up.'

But the African sister stood still. 'When we are not working,' she said with difficulty, 'I would be pleased if you call me Agnes, and if I can call you Julie.'

'I will be very pleased too,' Julie replied, touched more than she would have thought possible, knowing that in the older woman's culture this meant a great deal.

And somehow she had the feeling that Agnes Nguli's friendship was going to mean a great deal to her, here in the mission hospital.

CHAPTER SEVEN

EVERY day now, the clouds piled up in the heavy sky, and often thunder rolled, but still no rain came.

'When the rains do come, there will be much—the old men in my village say so,' Agnes Nguli's niece Thandi said when she and her baby left the hospital.

'Go well, Thandi,' Julie said to her—not brave enough yet to try to give the traditional greeting in the girl's own language.

'Thank you, Sister Norton, and may it go well with you too.' Thandi put her arms around her aunt and hugged her. 'Thank you, Aunt Agnes—you will come and visit us soon, and see how your godson is growing?'

'I will, Thandi,' Agnes Nguli promised.

When the small cart Thandi's young husband had brought to take his wife and his baby son back over the hills was out of sight, she turned to Julie.

'He is my godson, Julie,' she said quietly, 'but I think if it had not been for you we might not have had him.'

'He's certainly well recovered from any birth trauma,' Julie pointed out. She smiled. 'I've seldom seen a baby take so well to knowing how to go about getting his food!'

'Yes, he is a greedy little boy,' the African woman agreed fondly. 'Thandi will be bringing him to the mother and baby clinic, it will be interesting to see how he grows.' She looked up at the sky. 'At least there is no river between their village and the hospital, so even when the rains come she will be able to reach here.'

Everyone seemed certain that the rains this year would

be exceptionally heavy. Even David said, one night after dinner, that he hoped he wouldn't have any problem getting his children here.

'When do they arrive, David?' asked Julie, very conscious of Rob's eyes on her.

'On Friday,' said David. He glanced across at Rob. 'All right if I take the whole day, Rob? I'll drive into Umtata early, organise the supplies and pick up Timothy and Clare, then get back before it's dark.'

'I'll check that list again,' Rob said. 'We'll phone it through on Thursday, that might save you a bit of time too.'

Julie, finishing her coffee, had the definite feeling that Rob was looking for something more from her.

'You must be looking forward to seeing the children, David,' she said.

'I am,' he replied. 'I've missed them—and even a couple of months can make such a difference at that age. Clare has started ballet now—we'll probably be treated to a ballet concert from her. And Timothy is into karate, no doubt there'll be demonstrations of that too.'

He stood up.

'If you need any supplies, let me have a list too, will you, Julie?'

We're so polite with each other, so formal, Julie thought sadly when he had gone. I ask polite questions, David answers them, and that's all.

And yet what more could there be between us now? Other than memories. And no one, she thought with sudden determination, can take these memories from us!

'You're looking very fierce, Julie,' Rob remarked from the other side of the table.

'Sorry—I didn't mean to,' she replied, with an effort.

Unexpectedly, he put one hand over hers on the table. 'Don't you worry, now, girl dear,' he said, and the gentle concern in his voice, the unexpected other side to this man, brought a treacherous tightness to her throat.

'You know something, Rob Kennedy,' she said, not quite steadily, 'just when I'm feeling angry with you—because of the things you say to me—you do or say something that somehow isn't in character. And I don't quite know how to handle it.'

His hand tightened over hers, imprisoning it. 'And how do you know what is in my character and what isn't?' he asked her, and although there was warm teasing in his voice his eyes were dark and serious. 'You don't give yourself a chance to get to know the real Rob Kennedy, now do you?'

Julie drew her hand away and stood up. 'I'm not sure that I trust the real Rob Kennedy,' she said lightly.

He stood up too, and looked down at her. 'I sometimes wonder, Julie, if it's yourself that you dare not risk trusting,' he murmured.

'Goodnight, Rob,' she said quickly.

'Goodnight, Julie darlin',' Rob replied, and the disturbing deep laziness in his voice, the underlying laughter, made her hurry out so quickly that she bumped into Monika Jansen, just coming in.

'Oh—sorry, Monika,' she apologised. 'I'm always in too much of a hurry.'

'It certainly looks like it,' the German nurse returned coolly. 'Oh, you are leaving too, Rob? So I must eat my late supper alone.'

As Julie hurried out, she heard Rob say—and she thought there was resignation in his voice—that he did have time for another cup of coffee.

It disturbed her more than she wanted to admit to herself that Monika Jansen so clearly disliked and resented her. If the hospital had been bigger, if there had been more people on the staff, perhaps it wouldn't have mattered so much to her. And although she and Monika hadn't yet worked together there were so many occasions when they met—in the dining-room, in the corridor beside their rooms, up at the mission—that she was constantly brought up short by Monika's obvious hostility.

'Give her time,' Agnes Nguli said, when Julie talked to her about this. 'She has a number of reasons to resent you, Julie—or at least in her own eyes she does—and especially now that Elsa makes no secret of thinking that you are a very good nurse it is more difficult for her.'

'Everyone else is so friendly, I suppose that makes it more obvious,' Julie said. Then she smiled. 'Anyway, what right have I to expect that everyone should like me and be my friend?'

'Because you are a nice girl, Julie,' the older woman replied seriously. Then she smiled too. 'And because you are a friendly person yourself.'

Because it was easy to talk to the African nurse now, and because Julie respected her common-sense approach, she told her, a little diffidently, that she was worried about Patience.

'I don't know what it is,' she admitted, 'in many ways, she's working just as hard as she always did, she's just as cheerful, just as obliging—and yet—I don't know, Agnes, there's something different about her.'

What it was, Julie discovered the day David went to collect his children.

Patience had gone for lunch early, and when she hadn't come back to let Julie go Julie went to the door to look for her. There was no sign of the young black girl coming across the dusty courtyard, and this surprised her, for Patience usually cut her lunch hour short, if Julie still had to go. Then, at the far corner, under the big baobab tree, she saw the gleam of a white uniform. Curious, she stayed where she was, and a few moments later Patience came out from the shade, turning to wave to a young man.

It was Simon, Julie realised, the young man who had had to have the fish-hoek removed from his hand.

Patience, running now, realised that Julie had seen her. 'Oh—I am so sorry, Julie, I am late,' she said breathlessly.

'It's all right, there's still time for me to go,' Julie replied. And then, because it was better brought out into the open, 'I didn't know you knew Simon, Patience.'

Patience's lashes covered her eyes. 'I did not know him until he came back to have his dressing changed,' she said softly. 'But now I know him, and—oh, Julie, we are liking each other very much!'

Julie couldn't help smiling, the girl was so happy, and so naïve. 'I'm glad to hear that, Patience,' she said, relieved to know just what it was that had been making her young assistant seem so different. She hesitated and then said casually, 'This is your first boyfriend, Patience?'

'Oh, yes,' Patience replied earnestly. 'And for Simon, I am the first too.' She looked at the clock on the wall. 'You must go, Julie, and have lunch.'

And that, Julie thought, amused, tells me that she doesn't need me to say anything more. No advice needed. But, all the same, Patience is very young, and I will just keep an eye on her, she decided.

She heard the Land Rover return in the middle of the afternoon, and from the labour ward she could hear the excited sound of children's voices, but she was in the middle of a delivery, and her patient had had to have an episiotomy, so by the time Julie had completed the stitching and was able to glance out into the courtyard, there was no one there. She wasn't sure, in fact, whether she felt disappointed or relieved.

She wanted to see David's children, but at the same time she knew she felt a reluctance to see him as a father. This was what Rob had told her she had to do, and she had an uneasy feeling that he was right. But she wasn't entirely sorry that the moment had been delayed.

But only delayed until suppertime. As she pushed open the door of the dining-room, she saw David first. He was smiling, and his hair was less tidy than it usually was, and he looked younger, more relaxed, more carefree. More like the young doctor she had fallen in love with all those years ago, she thought, and the sharp pang of that thought dismayed her.

The little boy sitting opposite him must be like his mother, she decided. He was fair-haired and blue-eyed, and there was a dusting of freckles on his nose. But the little girl—her breath caught in her throat, because this small daughter of David's was so very like him. Not as blonde as her brother, and her eyes were grey, her small face serious, now, as she struggled to wield the large fork and knife.

For a moment Julie stood still, and the small family cameo engraved itself in her mind. Then David looked up and saw her.

'Hello, Julie,' he said, and stood up. 'Come and meet Timothy and Clare. This is Sister Norton, you two—she and I knew each other a long time ago.'

'Before I was born?' Clare asked, with the absorbed self-interest of the very young.

For a moment, above the child's head, David's eyes met Julie's. 'Yes, Clare,' he said steadily. 'Before you were born.'

The little boy, Timothy, smiled. It was a shy smile,

but it lit up his small face. If he's like his mother, Julie found herself thinking, she must be very attractive.

'Do we have to call you Sister Norton?' Clare asked.

'Not if you'd rather call me Julie,' Julie told her, amused at the little girl's self-possession. She was six, David had said, and Timothy eight, but she seemed to be the spokesman for the two of them.

She sat down at the table beside them, glad that Rob wasn't here to see her first meeting with David's children.

'Was it bumpy on the plane?' she asked Timothy.

'Not until we were near Umtata,' he told her. 'The pilot said it was because it was stormy.'

'We were bumping into the clouds, you see,' Clare explained.

'Yes, I suppose you were,' Julie replied, not quite succeeding in hiding a smile. David, she saw, was having trouble too.

'Do you know what?' Timothy said, overcoming his shyness. 'The air hostess is a friend of Mummy's, and she took us to the pilot's cabin, to say hello to him!'

'You were very lucky,' Julie told him.

'And we stayed there for a long time,' Timothy said. 'And you should see all the instruments you need to fly a big plane like that!'

The door opened, and Rob came in. Both children jumped up from the table and ran to greet him. He swung Clare up on to his shoulder, and when he put her down he shook hands with Timothy.

'I can see you'd be much too heavy for me to lift you up,' he said. 'Sure and you're a lot bigger than you were last time, Timothy.'

'It's the karate,' the little boy told him seriously. 'It develops muscles. Can you do karate, Rob?'

Rob shook his head. 'No, I can't, but I'm hoping you

will show me one or two of the easier things I could do—
it could be useful.'

He sat down at the table, across from Julie. Just for a
moment his eyes held hers, and the warm, steadying
assurance of his glance helped her more than she would
have thought possible. And she could admit to herself,
now, that she was glad of that help. After this first
meeting it wouldn't be so bad, she would become accustomed to seeing David with the children, David as their
father.

And she would not allow herself to think that, if things
had been different, these children might have been hers.

The next night Julie went up to the mission after supper.
The children wanted her to play Snakes and Ladders
with them, but she had a letter from her father that she
wanted to tell Meg and Steve about, so she promised that
the following night she would play a game with them.

Once again peals of thunder rolled around the distant
hills, and far away she could see lightning. But still no
rain.

Meg's due date was in two weeks now, and Julie had
hoped that by now the baby's head would have engaged.

'I'm sure nothing's happened since last week,' Meg
told her. She put one hand on what had once been her
waistline. 'Helen says I would know if the baby had
dropped—and I'm sure he hasn't.'

'Come down tomorrow, and we'll give you a complete
check,' Julie suggested, following her friend into the big
room. She hesitated, knowing how Meg would take the
suggestion she was going to make.

'We were wondering—Rob and I—whether you
shouldn't just go to Umtata anyway,' she said, as they
were drinking coffee. 'If the rains should come, as

everyone seems to be sure they will, it could be a problem.'

Steve put down his coffee-cup and turned to his wife. 'Isn't that just what I was suggesting?' he said to her.

Meg smiled. 'I really don't want to be difficult,' she said, 'and if the baby's head were engaged I'd probably agree. But Faith has this cold, you see, and I don't want to take her to strange surroundings—I'll tell you what, as soon as her cold's better we'll go.'

Steve shook his head. 'That isn't good enough,' he told her decisively. 'I'd say, better or not, you go in a couple of days.'

'I would agree,' Julie said. 'Anyway, we'll see what your check-up shows tomorrow.' She took her father's letter from her pocket. 'Look, I hope you don't mind, but I told my folks what you're hoping to do, about sending one or two people to the Valley Trust to learn about agriculture and nutrition and come back here to teach other people. Well, my father told his Rotary Club, and they decided this was something they would like to help with, so he'll give me details soon, but it looks as if you could begin to decide which two of your people you're going to send.'

Meg hugged her. 'Julie, how wonderful!' she exclaimed, delighted. 'There was just no way we were going to be able to send anyone for ages. Steve, who do you think we should send?'

'We'll have to think about that,' Steve said. 'Julie, this is marvellous! Can I write to your father to thank him?'

'Wait till he gives us more details, Steve,' Julie said. She finished her coffee and stood up. 'I'd better get back down. And tomorrow night I've promised to play Snakes and Ladders.'

'I must bring Faith down to see Timothy and Clare,' Meg said. 'She loves them.'

Julie shook her head. 'If Faith is well enough to play with the children,' she said severely, 'she's well enough to be taken to Umtata! See you tomorrow, Meg.'

'Are you sure you'll be all right?' Steve Winter said doubtfully, as he stood at the door with Julie. Anxiously he looked up as a jagged streak of lightning lit up the dark sky, followed almost immediately by a peal of thunder that seemed to be directly above them. 'I'll come down with you, Julie.'

'No, you won't,' Julie told him. 'I'll run down—it's only five minutes, Steve.'

He called something after her as she hurried off, but she couldn't hear him because there was more thunder. And halfway down the hill the heavens opened, and the rains began with all the force that had been building up and threatening. Within a minute, Julie was soaked. Rain ran down her face, and she could feel her thin shirt clinging to her.

It was impossible to run, for already the dusty road was muddy and slippy. Gasping for breath, Julie slowed to a walk. She had never been out in a storm like this, and she was more than a little afraid.

And then suddenly a figure loomed out of the darkness, and arms held her close.

'You silly little fool!' Rob shouted, above the thunder. 'Are you trying to get yourself killed? You and your darned independence!'

She didn't care how much he shouted at her, she thought thankfully, as his arm held her tightly against him. He was carrying a torch, and although the light of it was feeble it did show them where the road was.

Battered and soaked as they both were, it seemed to take an eternity to reach the first hospital building, and to find comparative peace in its shelter.

'Fortunately, Steve rang to tell me you were on the

way down,' Rob said, and there was still anger in his voice. 'What good would you be to anybody, do you think, and you struck by lightning?' His voice changed, and in the glow of the light on the corner of the building, he looked down at her. 'Or maybe,' he said, 'catching your death of cold from pneumonia.'

Julie, looking down at herself as well, felt her cheeks grow warm, as she realised that her thin shirt was completely soaking, clinging to her, and almost transparent.

'Get inside, for heaven's sake, and have a hot bath,' he told her, and there was amusement in his voice now. 'You could be doing with someone to come with you and see that you do it, and to rub your hair dry for you, but I don't think the mission committee would be thinking it was a good enough reason for me to come in with you.' He gave her a friendly pat on her behind. 'So be off with you, and get that bath going.'

At the door to the women's quarters, Julie turned round. 'Thank you for coming to meet me, Rob,' she said.

Another peal of thunder drowned out his reply, but as she closed the door he blew her a kiss, jauntily.

Ridiculous man! Julie told herself.

But as she hurried along to her room she couldn't help smiling.

CHAPTER EIGHT

ALL through the night, the torrential rain fell.

Julie, wakened from time to time by the thunder or the lightning, padded to her window and looked out, and each time the rain was a solid wall of water.

By morning it had lessened to an ordinary steady downpour, and there was no more rain. But the heavy lowering clouds promised a great deal more still to come.

The road up the hill to the mission had become a morass, and when Meg Winter phoned to ask if she should try to come down, Julie confirmed with her that she felt just as she had felt the night before.

'See what it looks like in the afternoon,' Julie said. 'The last thing we want is any complications, and I don't think even the four-wheel-drive Land Rovers could make it the way it is right now.'

In fact, it was the next morning before Steve managed to drive the Land Rover down the hill, to bring Meg.

'We left Faith with Helen,' said Meg, when Julie asked about the little girl. 'She loves Helen's baby—we're hoping it means she'll take easily to our own.' She looked up at Julie, who was examining her now. 'What is it?' she asked, quite sharply for Meg, and Julie knew that this time she hadn't been able to hide her change of expression.

'The head is engaged,' she told her friend. And well down too, she thought, but she didn't say that. 'Relax, Meg, I haven't finished.'

When she had taken off her gloves, and taken Meg's blood-pressure, she helped her to sit up.

'We don't need to get too excited,' she said, as casually as she could. 'Often with first babies it's at least a week, even longer, after the head engages. But there's no doubt, Meg, that you must go to Umtata now.'

Meg's blue eyes met her own steadily. 'Then you haven't heard?' she asked.

'Heard what?' Julie asked.

'That the river is down,' Meg said quietly. 'We can't get through until it goes down.'

'How long does it usually take to go down?' Julie asked.

Meg shrugged. 'Depends on how much rain comes down from the mountains,' she said. 'Two years ago we were cut off for a week.'

A week! Julie thought, dismayed. A week might be too long for Meg, with this baby's head as firmly engaged as it was.

'Well,' she said briskly, 'we'll just have to hope it isn't as long this time, won't we?'

She had just waved goodbye to Meg and Steve, watching the Land Rover fighting for traction in the muddy morass the courtyard had become, when Rob came hurrying across from the general ward, a huge umbrella over his head.

'Oh, I've missed them,' he said breathlessly, as he reached her. 'I was held up doing the anaesthetic for David to set that fractured tibia. How's Meg?'

'The head is engaged,' Julie told him. 'And Meg tells me the river is down, and she can't get to Umtata.'

His eyes met hers. 'She could have a week,' he said, after a while.

'She could,' Julie agreed.

And the words between them didn't need to be said—and again, she might not.

'Look,' said Rob, then, 'it isn't the end of the world if

we have to deliver the baby here. There aren't any other problems, on the face of it. How was her blood-pressure today?'

'Normal,' Julie told him. 'You're right, Rob, I know that, but she is an older mother, and she's at risk because of that, and with her history——'

It wasn't right, she knew, to become personally and emotionally involved with a patient, but she couldn't help it this time; Meg had become her friend, and she knew how much this baby meant to them, and she couldn't bear the thought of anything going wrong.

'I'd better get back to work,' she said, turning away. But not before the Irish doctor had seen the gleam of tears in her eyes, she realised, as he put his hand on her arm.

'Julie,' he said, and the unexpected gentleness of his voice unnerved her, 'don't you be making it worse for yourself, now. Remember, Meg has never carried a baby to term before. And you told me yourself even last time that the baby is a good enough size to come into the world. Maybe the river will go down, maybe she'll be able to get to Umtata, but—if she can't, we'll do everything in our power to see that she has her baby safely. Chin up, now!'

She stood in the doorway until the big black umbrella had reached the other side of the courtyard, and then she turned and went back to her ward. Rob was right, there was no problem either with Meg or with the baby, so there was no point in worrying. As he said, the river might go down.

But the river didn't go down. Most of their patients were able to come over the hills to them, and the two Julie had been worried about, knowing both were due, reached her the next day and both babies were delivered safely. Only three of her expected ten mothers-to-be arrived for the weekly clinic, and that didn't surprise her at all, for every day the rain kept coming steadily.

Each day either she or Rob saw Meg, and each day they were both only too glad to report that nothing more was happening.

Julie had had her promised evening of games with Timothy and Clare, and when it was her day off a few days later she went over to have a late breakfast, and found the children sitting at the far end of the big table, doing a jigsaw puzzle. Their faces lit up when she went in.

'Daddy said we'd be better to stay down here,' Timothy explained. 'He's going to be busy today, and he won't have time to come up and down to the house.'

'And he doesn't want us to get wet, or maybe fall, coming down by ourselves,' Clare said.

By unspoken consent they left the jigsaw and moved up beside her.

'I suppose you've had breakfast?' Julie asked.

The children nodded.

'Why are you late?' Clare asked, her chin resting on her small hands. 'And why don't you have your uniform on?'

'Because this is my day off,' Julie explained.

'I thought so,' Clare said, satisfied. Her grey eyes were wide and innocent. 'And with the rain, you won't be able to go anywhere, will you?'

'No, I won't,' Julie agreed, hiding her amusement, for she could see very well where this was leading.

'You could play with us,' Clare suggested. 'We could all keep each other company, on a drefful day like this.'

'Dreadful,' Timothy muttered under his breath, but his small sister chose not to hear him. Her eyes were fixed unwaveringly on Julie.

'What do you think we could do?' Julie asked.

'Oh, lots of things,' Clare said eagerly. 'We could play Snakes and Ladders again, or you could read to us, or we could do that jigsaw puzzle, but I don't really like jigsaws very much.'

'That's because she's isn't very good at them,' Timothy explained to Julie, as one adult to another.

'I am too!' Clare returned indignantly. 'But this one is a very hard one, it has too much sky in it.' Her small face brightened. 'We could do a concert for you, Julie. I could dance for you, and Timothy could show you some karate.'

'You can't do karate with just one person,' Timothy pointed out reasonably.

'You could pretend,' his sister told him. 'Don't you think that would be a good idea, Julie, to have a concert?'

'I think it's a great idea,' Julie replied. 'Tell you what, I'll go back and make my bed, and tidy my room, and you two can practise. Then you'll be ready when I come back.'

She had meant to have a day on letter-writing, for although she had written regularly to her parents there were a few friends she'd promised to write to as well, and by now they must be thinking she had forgotten them. But it would be a long day for the children, she could see that, not being able to get out at all, and if they did their 'concert' for her, they might be content to read or do the jigsaw later—even if there was too much sky in it, she thought, amused.

When she got back to the dining-room, leaving her big umbrella outside, the children were waiting for her.

'Me first!' said Clare. Suddenly her small face was tragic. 'But we don't have music, and I can't dance with no music.'

Julie thought quickly. 'I'll go and get my tape recorder,' she suggested. 'I don't think I have any proper ballet music with me, but I'm sure there's something you can dance to.'

The only tape she had that was remotely suitable was Offenbach's *Gaieté Parisienne*, and although Clare looked doubtful, as she listened to the music her face cleared and soon she was dancing, her chubby arms raised above her head with a grace that promised a great deal, and her small face intent as she concentrated on her foot positions, and then on the simple steps she had been taught.

When she had finished, Julie and Timothy both clapped loudly, and Clare, her hands holding the legs of her jeans, curtsyed.

'That was lovely, Clare,' Julie said, meaning it.

'Thank you,' the little girl replied, and Julie was amused again at her self-possession. 'But it looks much nicer with my proper ballet shoes on.'

'And a tutu,' Julie agreed.

'I haven't never had one yet,' Clare said. 'But when we have our real concert Mummy will make one for me, and it will stand out right to here.'

'I think you'll look very pretty in it,' Julie said.

'I think so too,' Clare agreed.

Julie became conscious of Timothy's silence. 'It will be difficult without someone else, Timothy, but couldn't you sort of show us some karate, and explain?' she suggested.

The little boy looked doubtful, but she persuaded him, and she and Clare sat in the two chairs for the audience, and he went to the middle of the floor.

'You have to stand like this,' he told them, considerably more self-consciously than Clare. 'And you hold your hands like this.'

'Show us how you fall, Timothy,' Clare said imperiously.

It needed three demonstrations before Julie and Clare had grasped the finer points of the right way of falling, and after that Clare, tired, Julie suspected, of not being the focal point of attention, had to have a go at falling too. By the time they had done that, and put some more sky into the puzzle, it was only half an hour till lunchtime, and Julie suggested that they could all sit and read.

'We have that at school sometimes, silent reading,' Timothy agreed, but the idea didn't appeal as much to Clare.

'You could tell us about your house, and your mummy and daddy, and things like that,' she suggested to Julie.

'Do you have any dogs or cats?' Timothy asked eagerly.

Giving in, Julie told them about Tess, the old golden Labrador, and Sooty, the black cat who liked to go for a walk too, when Tess was taken out.

'We have a dog too,' Timothy told her. 'His name is Tiger, but he isn't really fierce.'

'What kind of dog is he?' asked Julie.

'Not any special kind, but he's a very nice dog,' Timothy assured her. 'Daddy wanted a dog with a—with a—pedigree, but Mummy said let's take a norphan dog, and that's what Tiger is, a norphan.'

'But he's very cuddly,' Clare put in. 'When he lies down you can roll all over him, and he doesn't mind one bit.' She turned to her brother. 'Timothy, we'll bring that photo of Tiger to let Julie see. What will we do now, Julie?' And without waiting for an answer, 'Do you know any poems, like maybe "The Owl and the Pussy-Cat"?'

Julie was still taking in the thought of David wanting a dog with a pedigree, and Sarah holding out for a 'norphan' dog instead. There was something in that that somehow changed the mental picture she had of the girl David had married.

'"The Owl and the Pussy-Cat"?' Clare suggested.

'I remember some of it,' Julie said, after a moment, and with the children sitting crosslegged on the floor beside her she began the once-familiar verses.

'The Owl and the Pussy-Cat went to sea
In a beautiful pea-green boat.
They took some honey, and plenty of money,
Wrapped up in a five-pound note.'

She hesitated, and from the doorway Rob Kennedy's voice joined in:

'The Owl looked up to the Stars above
And sang to a small guitar——'

Both children jumped to their feet.

'Rob, Rob, we've had a lovely time!' Clare told him. And almost in the same breath, 'Was the Owl's small guitar like your guitar, Rob?'

Julie looked at him. 'I didn't know you played the guitar, Rob,' she said.

He smiled down at her, his dark blue eyes warm, and she wondered how long he had been standing in the doorway.

'Like I tell you, girl dear, there is a great deal you don't know about me. And if Albert Schweitzer could be having his organ, surely I can be having my guitar? I'll play it for you some time. I could come and serenade you, but there would be two dangers. First, that Monika would be very disapproving, but second, that she might be thinking she was the one I was serenading!'

Clare tugged at his hand. 'I danced for Julie,' she told him. And then, generously, 'And Timothy did some karate for her.'

'But it isn't easy to do karate just yourself,' Timothy explained quickly.

The young girl who helped in the kitchen came in then and began to set out cutlery on the long table. Rob suggested to the children that they should go and wash their hands before lunch, and took them out into the corridor to head each one in the right direction.

'Shouldn't I go with Clare?' queried Julie.

He shook his head. 'She would tell you, I'm sure, that she's a big girl—she's six,' he said. 'They're nice kids, aren't they, Julie?'

'Yes, they are,' Julie replied, her voice low, for she knew very well the things he wasn't saying.

He put both hands on her shoulders. 'You're pretty nice yourself, spending all this time with them,' he said, and the warmth in his voice pleased her absurdly. 'You know,' he murmured, 'I've always had fairly strong principles about professional behaviour, but I'm thinking it would be different now, your being off duty today, would it not?'

Before she knew what he was thinking of, he was kissing her, his lips warm on hers, his arms gently but inexorably drawing her closer to him. Too close, Julie thought, dazed and bemused, for at any moment anyone might come in.

She drew back, knowing very well that she was reluctant, that she would rather have stayed in his arms and let herself respond as her whole body longed to.

This is ridiculous, she told herself. And——

'This is getting to be too much of a habit,' she said, trying to sound severe, but not succeeding, because somehow it was difficult to keep her voice steady.

'I was thinking much the same,' Rob agreed, unrepentant.

She felt, then, the sudden tension in his body, still so close to hers, and she turned round. David stood in the

doorway, and she was certain by the remote stillness of
his face that he had seen her in Rob's arms.

'I believe we've missed a grand morning's entertain-
ment, David,' Rob said easily. 'Clare has been dancing
for Julie, and Timothy has been demonstrating karate.'

It was a moment before David spoke. 'That was very
kind of you, Julie, to give up your time off to entertain
them,' he said politely.

Rob had made no effort to move back, and so Julie
moved, taking two steps back from him. For a moment,
there was a flicker of—could it be hurt? she wondered,
taken aback—in his eyes, then he recovered. The children came back then, and soon Monika and Agnes Nguli
came in, and in the noise and the talk Julie told herself
that she had imagined that look.

But she certainly hadn't imagined that David had seen
her in Rob's arms, for in the next few days it was all too
clear that he was avoiding her. It shouldn't have bothered
her, she told herself, for after all this was what she herself
had decided was best, for her and for David. But it hurt,
all the same.

There was still no possibility of getting Meg to the
State hospital in Umtata, for not only was the river close
to them in full flood, but they heard on the radio that the
bridge further on had been swept away.

'What about a helicopter?' Julie asked Rob, but he
shook his head, and told her that he had spoken to the
hospital administrator the day before, and the only
available helicopter was being used to take food to remote
areas which were completely cut off.

'They're working on the repairs to the bridge,' he told
her. 'For what that is worth, as far as Meg is concerned,
because I doubt very much if they will have it operational
in time. And there is still the river in flood, before she
gets to the bridge.'

The next day, Julie, finishing her charts in the small duty-room, looked out of the window to see the Land Rover from the mission pulling up outside the maternity ward. A moment later Steve Winter hurried out, and then helped Meg out.

Julie left her charts and went to the door to meet them. Steve was carrying a small suitcase, and although Meg smiled Julie could see that she was in considerable discomfort.

'Well, it looks as if this baby isn't prepared to wait,' she said, and her voice was strained.

Julie told Steve to wait in the duty-room, and took Meg through. A swift examination confirmed that the baby was indeed well on the way. And in something of a hurry too, Julie thought, but she didn't say that.

'Everything is fine,' she told Meg. 'The baby's heartbeat is good and strong, and you're coming along nicely. Now, we'll just get you ready, and then Steve can keep you company. You're lucky, you can have the labour ward all to yourself!'

As soon as Meg was ready, and in a hospital gown, Julie sent Patience through to tell Steve he could come. She could see how anxious he was, and she told him quickly that everything was coming along nicely.

'What are you doing now?' Steve asked, sitting down beside Meg.

'Checking the baby's heartbeat, and it's fine,' Julie told him. 'Look, Steve, each time she has a contraction, you can help by rubbing her back like this.'

'It helps—just having you here,' Meg said, with difficulty. Her hair lay in damp tendrils on her forehead, and Julie took a cool cloth and wiped it. Then, her voice low, she asked Patience to go and find out if Dr Kennedy could come.

'You're doing fine, Meg,' she reassured her friend.

'That's it, don't fight the contractions, they're helping your baby to come. Go with them, and breathe the way we practised.'

This baby, she realised, was going to be here very soon.

'Well, well, things are really happening, are they?'

She turned round.

Rob was at the door. He was smiling, but she knew that he had taken in all that was happening immediately. And she thought that in spite of all the times she had done deliveries with no doctor there, this time she was only too glad to see him there, to know that they would be working together.

'Need any help, Sister Norton?' he asked her, and now the smile had reached his eyes.

'Yes, thank you, Dr Kennedy,' she replied thankfully.

CHAPTER NINE

IT WAS strange, Julie thought afterwards, how well she and Rob worked together, as if they had been doing this for years, Rob hardly having to give her any instructions for she knew what he wanted her to do.

Meg's labour was hard, but short, and as the baby's head crowned, Julie thought that after all their concern this birth was not going to have any problems.

'Another push, Meg,' Rob urged. 'That's it—good girl! Wait—stop pushing.'

There was only one moment when Rob's eyes met Julie's, as they both saw the cord looped round the baby's neck. Julie herself had on a few occasions had to deal with this, and she knew that it was possible to ease the cord gently over the baby's head. If this couldn't be done, the cord could be cut between forceps, but she knew, as she reached for the forceps without needing to be asked, that Rob wouldn't do this unless he had to, because of the danger of cutting off the baby's oxygen supply.

'No time,' Rob said under his breath, and in the next second the baby's shoulders appeared.

Fortunately, Julie realised, neither Meg nor Steve knew at that moment that their baby was in danger. And, even as she began to plan in her mind the immediate steps necessary if the baby suffered from oxygen deprivation now, in one smooth and skilful movement Rob slipped the cord over the baby's shoulder and delivered him through the loop.

'You've got your son, Meg,' he said, and Julie knew

that she was the only one who could sense the overwhelming relief in his voice as she clamped the cord, and then handed the baby to Meg.

'And that's a good pair of lungs he's got,' he commented to Steve, as the scarlet-faced baby gave a yell of outrage.

Julie helped Meg to sit up further, as she held her baby in her arms. Steve, moving closer, touched the baby's cheek gently with one finger. Neither of them said anything, but for a moment their eyes met over their baby's head.

In all her years as a midwife, Julie had never been able to take this moment of birth for granted, but this baby's birth was very special. She turned away, unwilling to intrude on the closeness between Steve and Meg and their baby.

Rob looked down at her, and she knew that he had been as moved as she was.

'You did a superb job, Dr Kennedy,' she said, not quite steadily. 'I've read in Maggie Myles that that's possible, but I've never seen it done.'

'I've only done it once before myself,' Rob admitted. 'And that was with my old prof in Edinburgh standing by.' His blue eyes darkened. 'I suppose,' he said softly, 'you will be telling me these are happy tears?'

Gently he wiped away the tears she hadn't realised were running down her cheeks.

'I'm sure Meg must be dying for a cup of tea, are you not, Meg?' he asked then, turning back to the bed.

'I'll get Patience to make some,' Julie said. 'Then we'll get you and your son smartened up a bit, Meg.'

'I didn't even have any stitches,' Meg said wonderingly. Reluctantly she handed the baby, wrapped in a receiving blanket now, to Julie.

He doesn't even need suction, Julie thought, looking

down at the tiny dark-haired baby boy. She knew very well that he couldn't see her, but it did seem that he was looking right at her, and she couldn't help smiling to him. And then, looking up, she found Rob Kennedy's eyes on her, dark blue and unsmiling, and with something new, something very disturbing in them.

'I'll see about that tea,' she said briskly, and went to call Patience.

It was only later, when she went to the door with Steve, that they saw that the rain had stopped, and over the distant hills there was a faint but definite rainbow.

'I'm not superstitious,' Steve said, as he got into the Land Rover, 'but I can't help thinking that's a very good sign, both for the end of the rain and for our baby.'

He was right on both counts.

There was no more rain, and the baby—to be called Robin, in honour of Rob, they had decided—never looked back, after his difficult start. Little Faith didn't show more than a passing interest in him, but that, Meg felt, was healthy. But when Steve brought her with him to take Meg and the baby home, the toddler shook her head when she saw Meg coming out with baby Robin in her arms.

'Not tum,' she said definitely.

Meg handed the baby to Julie.

'Darling, the baby has to come with us, he's our baby,' she said gently. 'You're going to help Mummy to look after him.'

Little Faith was still frowning, her lower lip trembling.

'I think this is the time, rather than later,' Meg said to Steve. She opened her bag and took out a small baby doll, wrapped up in a blanket.

'Look, Faith, this is your baby,' she said. 'Mummy has a baby, and you have a baby. Let's take our babies home and put them to bed, shall we?'

And as the Land Rover drove off, Julie could see that the little girl was doing her best to hold her doll just as her mother was holding baby Robin.

By the end of that week the river was down, and passable, and although the bridge hadn't been repaired there was a ferry to take cars and people across, so the way was open again to Umtata. David, taking the children with him, went through for supplies, and reported that in spite of the problems the heavy rains had brought people were very pleased, because the dams had filled up well.

Although Julie saw a fair bit of Timothy and Clare, and spent time off that she had with them, she found an excuse to leave any time David joined them. She wasn't sure whether she still felt uncomfortable because David had seen her in Rob's arms, or because there was a deep hurt at seeing him with his children, hearing them say Daddy. All she knew for sure was that she felt it was better for her to see as little of David as possible.

And so she was taken aback, when she left the dining-room one night, to find him waiting outside.

'Hello, Julie,' he said quietly.

'Oh—I thought you'd taken Timothy and Clare to put them to bed,' Julie said awkwardly.

'I did, and then I came back because I want to talk to you. Let's walk this way.'

And without giving her time to refuse he took her arm and led her to the path going down to the river. The sky was so clear now that the moonlight made it almost as bright as day.

David, feeling her resistance, looked down at her. 'I just want to talk to you, Julie,' he said quietly. 'Surely you won't grudge me that?'

There was nothing she could say in reply to that. But as they reached the corner she stopped.

'We can talk here,' she said.

'Do you feel safer with the hospital in sight?' he asked her. And without waiting for an answer, 'Julie, I don't know what you've heard about Sarah and me, but I'd like to get this clear. We're separated, by Sarah's choice, and that's why I'm here alone. She wanted this, and now she's got it, and although I certainly didn't come here with any intention of—becoming involved with anyone else, seeing you again, remembering what we were to each other, remembering how I—missed you—Julie, don't you feel too that we've been given another chance? All these years we've been apart—and now here we are, and——'

His voice was low now, and not quite steady.

'And it hurts like hell, Julie, to know you're avoiding me.'

They had stood in the moonlight the night he told her he was going to marry Sarah. It was a long time ago, but she remembered it very well.

She turned her head away. 'I don't think you have the right to say that, David. It just seems wiser for us not to see each other.'

His hand on her arm swung her round, and she could see that he was angry.

'And I don't suppose I have any right to do this either.'

He kissed her, his lips hard and demanding, his arms holding her close. So many times, through the years without him, she had dreamed of him kissing her again. And yet, now that it was happening, she had a strange, disembodied feeling. Almost, she thought later, as if it were happening to someone else.

And certainly not, she knew, the way she felt in Rob Kennedy's arms.

That thought, with all its disturbing implications, made her draw back from David's arms. He looked down at her for a long time in the moonlight, his eyes searching her face.

This is David, this is the man I once loved, the man I have never forgotten, Julie told herself.

He was tense, waiting, she knew, for her to move back into his arms.

'I'd like to go back now, David,' she said evenly.

Neither of them said anything as they walked back, and the short distance between them seemed like an unbridgeable chasm. When they reached the courtyard, she looked up at him.

'Goodnight, David,' she said, but he didn't answer.

And he hadn't, she realised, made any reference to Rob.

She thought, a few days later, reproaching herself, that it was her preoccupation with her own thoughts, her own feelings, that made her less aware of two things. One was that Clare wasn't very well. It was only when the little girl refused ice-cream, and said she wasn't hungry, that Julie looked properly at her and realised that Clare was listless, that her eyes were shadowed.

When the children had left the table, Julie asked David if Clare was ill.

'She doesn't seem to be really ill, but at the same time she doesn't seem herself,' David replied, with some reluctance. He looked across the table at Rob. 'Would you mind giving her a check-over tomorrow, Rob?'

'I'll be glad to,' Rob replied. 'After all, when a child doesn't want ice-cream, something must be wrong!'

The other thing that Julie reproached herself for not seeing earlier was the change in Patience. The young girl was doing her usual morning job of bathing the new babies, and Julie, checkng supplies beside her, realised suddenly that Patience wasn't singing as she usually did.

She was doing her job, and she was doing it as efficiently as always, but—something was lacking.

And now that she had noticed that, she saw that Patience hardly ever seemed to smile now, and where before she had walked as if her feet were hardly touching the ground, now there was a heaviness about her movements.

Once or twice Julie asked her if she was feeling all right, and each time the girl answered politely that she was well, thank you.

Then Julie found her crying in the sluice-room, and this time she refused to be put off.

'This is nonsense, Patience,' she said firmly. 'Come along to the duty-room, we'll have tea—there's nothing needing done on the ward for a little while—and you're going to tell me what's wrong with you.'

She made tea and put a cup down in front of the girl, then waited. And when Patience, rubbing the back of her hand childishly over her eyes was silent, Julie leaned forward and took both the girl's hands in hers.

'It's Simon, I suppose,' she said gently. 'Have you quarrelled, Patience?'

'No—not really,' Patience replied, with difficulty. And then, as if she had found the courage to speak, 'Oh, Julie, Simon does not want me to go away and learn how to be a nurse, he wants me to marry him, and come and live in his hut, and—and be a good native wife like his mother, like his sisters!'

'And you, Patience? What do you want?' Julie asked.

Patience shook her head. 'I do not know,' she said sadly. 'I do want to be Simon's wife, and—and I do not want him to find someone else, but I have wanted to be a nurse for so long. And—and this is why I am very unhappy, Julie, because I do not know what to do.'

Julie put her arms round the girl and held her close

while she cried. Then she poured more tea for them both, and wondered what to say, what to do.

'I don't know either, Patience,' she admitted at last. And as she said it, she knew what she would do, and her thoughts cleared. 'I'll tell you what, I'll speak to Dr Kennedy. He saw Simon the last time he was here, when he was discharged—maybe he could talk to him.'

That night, when she asked Rob, he looked a little dismayed.

'That's quite something you're asking, Julie,' he said, after a while. 'You know that Simon is the headman's son? They'll be expecting him to marry, and provide an heir.'

'You could just talk to him, maybe?' Julie asked. 'Try to get him to see it from Patience's point of view.'

Her hand was lying on the table, and Rob covered it with his own.

'Sure and it's a grand thing to feel that someone has such faith in you,' he said. 'I'll see what I can do, but I'm not making any promises.'

They were the last people in the dining-room, and as they walked to the door she asked him how his check of Clare had gone.

'I'm not too happy about her,' he admitted. 'Look, she isn't critically ill, or anything, but she does have a slight temp, she's headachey, she has some muscular pains——'

'Should she be kept in bed?' Julie asked, dismayed at the thought of the little girl in bed in the cottage David lived in.

Rob shook his head. 'I don't think she needs that,' he said. 'I'll keep an eye on her, see how she does. They're supposed to be going home next week, anyway.'

Julie had the next afternoon off, and since the weather

was clear and warm now, after all the rain, she took Clare and Timothy for a walk down to the pool at the river.

'We're not going to swim today,' she told them firmly before they set off. 'Firstly, Clare shouldn't swim, but also, the water must be very cold, after all the rain in the mountains.'

Timothy took his fishing-net with him, and this kept him occupied for a while, but Clare seemed too tired to want to take a turn. Julie sat quietly on the big flat stone with her, until Timothy decided he wasn't going to catch anything and he might as well give up.

'Did you bring that photo of Tiger to show Julie?' Clare asked, and Timothy opened his rucksack and took out a photo.

'There's Tiger,' Clare said proudly. 'Isn't he lovely?'

Tiger was large and woolly, and looked, Julie thought, more like a sheep than a tiger. But she agreed gravely that he was lovely.

'And of course this is your mummy with him?' she asked evenly.

Sarah Shaw was sitting on the grass, with one arm around the big dog. She was laughing, and her fair hair was blowing in the wind. She looked, Julie thought, young to be Timothy's and Clare's mother. She also looked very lovely. Sure of herself, of her place as David's wife, as the mother of these children. And yet she had wanted their separation——

You're being ridiculous, she told herself severely. This is only a snapshot, after all.

'I wish Mummy was here,' Clare said wistfully. 'I like it here, but I like it better at home.'

'But then you miss Daddy,' Timothy pointed out reasonably.

'I know,' Clare agreed. 'I like it the bestest when we're all together at home with Tiger.'

It was a moment before Timothy said anything. 'I do too,' he said at last, his voice low.

They had never before spoken of how they felt about their parents being separated, and Julie had somehow assumed that because they were very young they had just accepted it. But she could see now that, although they might have had to accept it, neither child was at all happy about the situation.

For a moment, indignation rose inside her, at what Sarah Shaw had done to these children by breaking up their family life.

'I think we'd better get back,' she said, more brusquely than she meant to. Clare clung to her hand as they walked back up to the hospital, and there was no doubt that she was really tired by the time they turned the last corner.

When dinner was over that night, Agnes Nguli told David, very firmly, that she was taking the children up to the cottage, to bath them and put them to bed.

'You can't bath me!' Timothy protested, horrified.

'All right, you will bath yourself,' the African nurse agreed equably. 'But I will bath this child here, and I will sit with her until she falls asleep.'

Quite meekly, David thanked her, and said goodnight to the children. I could have offered to do that before now, Julie thought, but there would be no possibility of any misunderstanding when Agnes Nguli made the offer.

'David,' Rob said abruptly, when Monika Jansen and Elsa Braun had left for the prayer meeting at the mission. 'I want to talk to you about Clare.'

Julie, unsure whether she should stay or go, half rose, but David gestured impatiently for her to sit down.

'What is it?' he asked.

'I've sent a blood test through to Umtata,' said Rob, his voice even now. 'I suspect glandular fever is a possibility. Now, you know and I know that that isn't an affair of life or death, but it is a long, debilitating illness, and Clare is only six, and I think——' He stopped.

Across the table, David's eyes met his. 'Yes?' he asked, his voice tight.

'I think you should send for Sarah,' Rob said flatly.

David turned away. 'That isn't necessary,' he said, and his voice was cold. 'If Clare is really ill, the best thing to do is to send her home. Sarah can look after her there.'

'Of course, that is an option,' Rob agreed.

Julie, looking from one man to the other, knew she had never seen the hostility between the two of them quite as much in the open as it was now.

'Myself, I think it's pretty heartless to put a small sick child on a plane and send her off on her own—all right, with her brother—when she could be comfortably looked after here, and I'm certain Sarah would rather make the journey than have Clare do it,' Rob said.

'Maybe we should wait until you get the result of the blood test,' David suggested.

'Oh, yes, we could do that,' Rob replied. 'And well you know that it will be a week until that comes through, and by that time Sarah could be here, and taking care of Clare, and I know that the child would feel better with her mother here.'

Across the table they faced each other, the two doctors.

'Any man with a real concern for his child would send for her mother,' Rob said.

All the colour left David's face. He stood up, and for a moment Julie thought he was going to strike Rob. But with a visible effort he restrained himself.

'I think you're making an unnecessary fuss,' he said, and now his voice was cool. 'But I'll go and phone Sarah now.'

He walked out of the room.

CHAPTER TEN

'YOU were pretty hard on David,' Julie said, when the silence between Rob and her had to be broken.

'I suppose I was,' Rob agreed, without a shade of repentance.

And there was something in his voice, in his eyes, that made her look at him more sharply.

'Do you really think Clare has glandular fever, Rob?' she asked him coolly.

He shrugged. 'She has most of the symptoms,' he pointed out. 'She's tired, she's listless, she's a little feverish, a little headachey—and, you know, I'm sure, that it's almost impossible to diagnose without a blood test. We certainly can't rule it out.'

'You're positive enough, though, to insist on her mother being sent for,' Julie said flatly.

'I didn't insist,' Rob returned. 'David took the decision himself.'

Julie stood up. 'You made it impossible for him to do anything else,' she said, and turned away.

Immediately Rob was on his feet, striding across the room to meet her at the door. His hands were hard on her shoulders.

'Does it bother you so much,' he said tightly, 'the thought of David Shaw's wife coming here? Does it spoil things for you?'

'You have no right to say that!' Julie flung at him, furious.

His hands dropped from her shoulders. 'No, I haven't,'

he agreed, and the unexpected and uncharacteristic weariness in his voice shook her more than she would have thought possible. 'I'm—sorry, Julie.'

His apology disconcerted her so much that she couldn't reply.

'What I see,' he said then, his voice low, 'is a little girl who's unwell. There may be a physical reason for this, or there may not. But whatever the results of that blood test I know—I know, Julie—that Clare will be better with her mother here. With both her parents here together.'

Her anger had gone. She couldn't help remembering David's children speaking, just the other day, about their parents being apart, and she couldn't forget the longing she had seen in them for the family to be together again.

'You can't interfere in people's lives just like that, Rob,' she said, not quite steadily. 'You can't push people around like that.'

For a moment he was taken aback. Then he recovered. 'Sometimes,' he said levelly, 'people need a hefty shove to make them see sense. Goodnight, Julie.'

He closed the door behind him then, with a firm finality that dismayed her. For a moment, foolishly, she wanted to run after him, to tell him that she did understand how little Clare felt, that she wasn't trying to come between David and his wife, that——

But she stood still, asking herself, bewildered, just why it mattered so much to hear what this maddening Irish doctor thought of her. And half afraid to try to answer that question.

Two days later Sarah Shaw arrived.

David had gone to Umtata to meet her, taking Timothy with him, and leaving Clare up at the mission station in Meg Winter's care. Clare adored little Faith, and she was fascinated by baby Robin, but Julie, glancing out the open window as David lifted Clare up into the Land Rover, saw that the little girl was very tearful.

'No, Clare, the journey is too long and too hot, when you're not well,' David said firmly. 'You can sit quietly with the children in Meg's play-group, and when Faith has a rest after lunch you'll have a rest too.'

'But I want to see Mummy,' Clare said shakily, as Timothy scrambled up to join her in the front seat.

'You'll see her later today,' her father told her. 'Now, we'll drop you, and then Timothy and I must be on our way.'

He glanced across then, and saw Julie at the window. It was too late for her to draw back, and she waved to the children, all too conscious that her cheeks were warm with colour.

'Sister!' Patience called from the ward, and she was glad to turn back, glad to have the reassuring routine to involve herself in.

The young African girl was still very quiet and subdued. Julie knew she should ask Rob if he had had the chance to talk to Simon, to see if there was any solution to the young man's unwillingness to let Patience train as a nurse. But she felt awkward and ill at ease with him now, and in many ways she was grateful that her maternity ward had had no emergencies, that his visits there had been routine and professional.

But I must talk to him, she told herself, seeing the shadows under the girl's dark eyes.

There were two unexpected admissions in the late afternoon, and although one woman delivered very quickly the other was obviously going to be some time. Julie sent Patience for early dinner, and it was well after seven when she hurried across the courtyard herself, knowing that Patience would call her when she was needed.

For a moment, as she stood outside the dining-room, she braced herself, sure that David would be back, that now, after all these years, she was at last going to meet the girl he had chosen instead of her.

'Julie,' Clare called, from her place beside Agnes Nguli, 'my daddy isn't here yet, with my mummy, but they're coming soon!'

'That's good, Clare,' Julie said steadily, conscious of Rob's eyes on her. 'You must be pleased that your mummy's coming.'

'Yes, I am,' Clare agreed. 'Rob said I'd feel better when my mummy came, but I think I feel better just knowing she's coming. But she can't bring Tiger, you know.'

'No, I don't suppose she can,' Julie replied, sitting down in the seat opposite Rob, because Mrs Nzama from the kitchen had set her plate down there.

'He's too big,' Clare told her. 'He'd need a whole seat to himself, so he stays with my gran and grandad instead, and he likes it there, 'cos they have Lulu, she's a French poodle, and she's tiny, but Tiger likes her.'

Agnes Nguli pointed out to the little girl that she'd eaten only half of her pink pudding, and while Clare was insisting that she'd had enough Elsa Braun, who was on night duty in the general ward, hurried off, and Monika Jansen left at the same time to go up to the mission station.

In the middle of all this activity, Julie looked across at Rob.

'It looks as if you were right, Rob,' she said, with some difficulty. 'The patient has improved already.'

Immediately his dark blue eyes lit up, and he leaned across the table, embarrassingly oblivious of the rest of the people in the room.

'I was thinking about what you said,' he said, his voice

low. 'And you're right, I shouldn't be thinking I can move people around as if they were on a chessboard. But it wasn't really like that, Julie, it was just—it seemed like a good chance to be doing something that would help everyone, instead of letting things drift.'

Julie was very conscious of Sister Nguli's eyes on them, on Rob's dark head so close to her own.

'I'd better hurry, I'm expecting Patience to send for me any time,' she said, not quite truthfully.

'I've been wanting to speak to you, but I've never found it easy to admit that I've been at fault,' Rob said disarmingly.

The two German nurses had gone, and the dining-room seemed all at once very quiet.

'Neither have I, Rob,' Julie admitted, and suddenly it didn't matter that the big African sister was obviously fascinated by this exchange—the only important thing was that the cool distance between them was gone, and once again they were friends.

Friends?

She had a sudden memory of Rob's lips warm on hers, of his arms around her, of the immediate response of her body to his.

'I hear the Land Rover!' Clare exclaimed, jumping down from the table. 'They're here! They're here!'

David had drawn up right at the door, and a moment later Timothy ran in.

'We had a flat tyre,' he said importantly, 'and Daddy had to change it, miles and miles from anywhere.'

'Mummy!' cried Clare, and she ran to the woman who had just come in.

Prettier, even, than her photograph, Julie thought, as the fair-haired young woman hugged the little girl. And in spite of the long, hot and dusty journey Sarah Shaw looked cool and well-groomed, in her cream trousers and her brightly striped shirt.

'You don't look too ill, my girl,' she said, a moment later, straightening up.

'I been ill,' Clare assured her. 'But I did feel better as soon as Daddy said you were coming, didn't I, Rob?'

'Certainly looks like it,' Rob agreed. He got up and went to the door, and kissed Sarah. 'Good to see you here again, Sarah.'

'Thank you, Rob,' Sarah said quietly. 'David said you thought I should come. Whatever the result of the blood test, you know I value your judgement.'

For a moment Julie had the strange feeling that there were things unsaid between David's wife and his colleague. And then Rob introduced her to Sarah.

'I'm so pleased to meet you, Julie,' Sarah said warmly. 'The children told me on the phone last week what fun they've been having with you. I appreciate your spending some of your precious off-duty time with them. I know what it means, from my own nursing days.'

Julie, on the point of exclaiming in surprise that she hadn't known that Sarah had been a nurse too, stopped herself. She didn't know, she realised, how much or how little Sarah knew about what she and David had been to each other ten years ago. And, until she did, it was surely better to be guarded.

'I've enjoyed being with them,' she said. 'Anyway, there isn't a great deal to do around here.'

Sarah Shaw laughed, a clear, unaffected laugh. 'You can say that again,' she agreed.

And Julie couldn't help wondering if that was why Sarah hadn't come here with David.

'Sister Norton, I think you come now,' Patience said breathlessly from the door, and Julie was glad to hurry

out with the girl across the courtyard, warm and still in
the summer evening.

The birth was straightforward, and soon the tiny baby
girl was tucked up in the cot beside her mother's bed.

'I think you and I can get ready to hand over to
Monika—she should be here soon,' Julie said to Patience,
realising suddenly that she was very tired. Monika Jansen
had asked for permission to go to a special church service
at the mission station that night, before coming on duty,
and Julie had agreed, glad that Monika had been able to
bring herself to ask even this small favour of her.

The ward lights were dimmed now, and the three
patients settling down for the night. And all three new
babies quiet, Julie thought thankfully, as she went to do
the usual hourly respiratory test on them.

And then, as she reached the third baby, she saw that
the tiny boy was limp and still, and even in the dim light
she could see that he was a bluish colour. He had been
perfectly healthy, there was no reason in the world——

Then her whirling thoughts stilled, and she remembered her textbook. Apnoea. A word and a condition
and, suddenly, terrifyingly real. In mild cases, you
flicked the baby's feet, and breathing might resume. If
this was ineffective, face-mask ventilation was applied
until spontaneous breathing recommenced. Report the
condition.

Gently but firmly she flicked the tiny feet. For an
eternity, nothing happened. Then, with a little gasp and
a shudder, the baby began to breathe again.

Afraid to move, afraid to take her eyes off him, Julie
said, her voice low—and steady, she hoped, for she
didn't want the mother to know what had happened,
'Patience, just go and ask Dr Kennedy to look in for a
moment, will you?'

By the time Patience came back with Rob, Julie knew

that the baby's breathing pattern was re-established. But she still felt that she dared not take her eyes off him.

'Anything I can do for you, Sister?' Rob asked, and she thought she had never been so glad to have the reassurance of his presence.

'Yes, thanks, Dr Kennedy,' she replied, and now she turned round. 'Just give little Nelson here a quick check, would you? We'll take him through to the labour ward—it's empty. Just settle down, Mrs Magana, we'll bring him back soon.'

She lifted the baby and carried him through, and as she laid him down on the bed she told Rob what had happened, then stood back while he examined the baby thoroughly.

'He seems to be all right now,' he said when he had finished. 'We've ruled out some of the causes—overheating, infection, hypoglycaemia. Very often, with apnoea, it's almost impossible to detect the cause, and it may never happen again. But I'd like to keep Nelson and his mother in for a few days, so that we can check the breathing pattern, watch the heart-rate, look out for cyanosis of the mucous membranes—any of these, and you sent for me right away.' Unexpectedly, then, he looked down at her. 'You all right, Sister?'

It took Julie a moment to recover from this. 'Yes, I'm all right now,' she said, with difficulty. 'It's just—outside of a textbook, I haven't seen this, and I thought I wouldn't be able to save him.'

'The flicking of the feet doesn't always work,' Rob agreed. 'Anyway, let's hope this was a one-off, and baby and Sister recover!' He glanced through the open door. 'Sounds as if that's Monika now—leave her to it, and come and have a cup of tea. You look as if you need it.'

Patience came through to take the baby back to his cot

beside his mother, and as she lifted him Rob put his hand on her arm.

'I haven't had the chance to talk to your young man yet, Patience, but I'm hoping to see him soon.'

'Thank you, Dr Kennedy,' Patience said, and she smiled shyly. 'I think if Simon will listen to anyone, it is to you.'

'Quite a responsibility,' Rob commented, as he and Julie walked back across to the dining-room, and she could hear the concern in his voice. 'I hope her faith in me isn't misplaced.'

At the door of the dining-room, he looked down at her.

'It's all right, girl dear,' he said, very gently. 'They've gone.'

And once again his perception of her feelings, and his sympathy, unnerved her.

'They went up to the cottage,' he said, casually now, as he switched the kettle on. 'Sarah felt it was time she got the children off to bed.'

While he made tea, he talked, lightly, of his time as a houseman in Dublin, and soon his outrageous—and, Julie was sure, quite untrue—stories had her smiling, and feeling herself again, after the stress of the last hour. And, she had to admit, the stress of David's wife arriving, of seeing David and her together, with their children.

'I feel much better now,' she told Rob, meaning it, when she had finished her tea. 'And I appreciate that you thought I needed sugar, but next time you make tea for me, no sugar, please.'

He took the empty cup from her. 'Well, now,' he said thoughtfully, and there was laughter in the dark blue of his eyes, 'surely you must know what we say in Ireland—tea and loving should be the same, hot and strong and sweet.'

'I don't believe half you tell me about Ireland,' Julie

told him, laughing. And then, unable to resist it, 'But the tea was good!'

'And that's a start, anyway,' Rob said cheerfully. He took both her hands and drew her to her feet. 'And now, Sister Norton, off to bed with you. Doctor's orders!'

For a moment, he put his arms around her and held her close to him. Nothing more. But when he let her go the warmth and the comfort of the brief, passionless embrace still seemed to enfold her.

And somehow, she found herself thinking in the next few days, to help her to take in her stride seeing Sarah and the children around the hospital, hearing Clare calling, 'Mummy, come and see this'—seeing, some-times, David and Sarah together, talking, the two fair heads close together.

The results of Clare's blood test were returned, and the test for glandular fever was negative. Julie wasn't there when David was told this, but Agnes Nguli said that of course he and Sarah were relieved.

'But it was still right to have Sarah come,' she said. 'The child needed her mother and, who knows, perhaps things might be better now for the two of them.'

There was something in the kindness in her dark eyes that made Julie wonder how much the older woman had guessed, or seen.

'I hope so,' Julie replied steadily.

The woman patted her hand, and although she said nothing more the unspoken understanding and sympathy brought a treacherous tightness to Julie's throat.

In some ways it was less hard than she had thought, and she realised that Rob had been right. She had needed to see David and Sarah together, to see them with their children. Perhaps Rob's 'hefty shove' in getting Sarah here had been the best thing for her.

But she was glad when Rob asked her if she could

come with him on a two-day visit to a distant clinic, glad of the chance to get away from Tabanduli for even that short time.

'It should be all right,' she agreed, checking the clinic folders. 'There's no one due to deliver for a few weeks, and of course David is here if anything does happen. What exactly do you want me to do?'

'First of all, help me,' Rob told her. 'There'll be dressings to change, maybe some stitching of wounds, there might be someone we have to bring back with us. But I'd like you to take the chance to talk to the women—the sort of talk you give your antenatal clinic patients, but these are women you could be reaching before they are pregnant—and, of course, I'd like you to talk to them about birth control. We'll have Depo-Provera with us, and anyone who agrees can have the three-month injection. But you might have some convincing to do first—the more rural the area, the more they feel that they have to have plenty of children.'

Their plan was to leave early the next morning, to make sure they would reach the most distant kraals before sunset, but there was an emergency appendectomy, and Rob had to assist with the anaesthetic, and then, when they had been driving for just over three hours, the Land Rover lurched to one side, and Rob had to change the punctured tyre.

'We can only afford one more puncture,' he told her cheerfully, wiping his hands on a rag before they got back in. 'What we really need, of course, is new tyres all round, and Steve is pushing that as an essential with the committee, but there's always a shortage of money.'

He glanced down at her as they started again. 'Steve was telling me that your father's Rotary Club is financing sending a couple of people for a training course at the Valley Trust,' he said. 'That should be a terrific help, having them come back and start sharing what they've learned.'

'I think he's decided on who's going,' Julie told him. 'There's a married couple who have been working at the mission station, and Steve thinks the best idea would be to send them together—they go off in a week or two, I believe.'

He hadn't talked about anything personal, and she was glad of that, for she didn't know how she would reply if he were to ask her how she felt, now, about David.

For so long, she realised painfully, he had been deep in her heart, in her memory, although she had never admitted it to herself. And meeting him at the hospital, seeing him daily, had somehow given her the feeling that the lost years were to be given back to her.

But somehow it wasn't possible for her to feel like that with Sarah and Timothy and Clare, real people—David's wife, David's children.

Lost in a reverie, she was thrown forward when they turned a corner and the Land Rover, its brakes protesting, screamed to a halt.

'What is it?' demanded Julie, bewildered, for the road had suddenly ended.

'Landslide,' Rob told her briefly. 'Looks as if it's just happened too.'

He climbed down and walked to the barrier of broken rock blocking the road. Then he looked up at the sky. The sun had already gone down, and there was no dusk here, no twilight—the African night would descend almost immediately.

'What are we going to do?' she asked, joining him.

He looked down at her. 'We can't do anything until morning,' he told her. 'Maybe, in daylight, we can clear enough rocks to let me drive round the side, but I dare not risk it in this light.'

The mountainside fell away sharply, and Julie knew he was right. But——that meant spending the night here, miles from anyone, miles from anywhere.

Just Rob and her.

Alone.

CHAPTER ELEVEN

ONE moment it was still daylight, although the sun had gone down behind the purple hills. And then, with startling swiftness, it was night—the warm African night that somehow seemed so different from night in the city, or even night at the hospital, where there were lights, people, sound, and movement.

Here everything was silent and still, and in spite of the warmth left over from the day Julie shivered.

'I'm not enough of a gentleman,' Rob said, glancing around, 'to offer to sleep outside. We'll have to share the Land Rover, and it's pretty cramped.'

They moved some of the medical supplies to the front, and managed to make enough room for both of them to stretch out.

'Here—you can have the blanket,' Rob said, and he handed Julie the only blanket.

They ate some of the sandwiches they had brought with them, and drank half the coffee from the big flask.

'I'm glad you told me not to wear my uniform to sit in the Land Rover,' Julie said, as she wrapped the blanket around her.

'You can change into it tomorrow, and look as if you've stepped straight out of the hospital—gives your patients confidence,' Rob told her.

'What about you?' Julie couldn't resist asking. 'Brought your white jacket?'

Rob shook his head. 'It doesn't matter what a doctor looks like,' he told her. 'But a nurse has to look like a nurse, come what may. Julie, we're going to have all the windows open, otherwise we won't be able to breathe. Does that make you nervous?'

'No,' she assured him, surprised. 'Why should it?'

But an hour later, lying awake in the warm darkness, listening to sounds where there had been no sounds, straining to hear distant rustlings, she had to admit that she didn't like the thought of the windows open all round, of the possibility of some animal coming close.

Rob seemed to be asleep, and in any case the last thing she was prepared to do was to admit that in fact she was extremely nervous, and very much on edge.

And then, not far away, there was a different sound. It was a low growl, Julie was certain. A lion—a leopard— she didn't know, and she didn't care.

'Rob!' she gasped, and without conscious thought she turned towards him. There was not a great deal of space between them, in any case, and the next moment his arms closed around her.

'What is it? Julie, what is it?'

She clung to him. 'I don't know—a lion, a leopard, somewhere out there, not far away.' She was close to tears, and she didn't care if he knew that.

He held her closer. 'Julie love, I don't think there are any lions around here—and firstly, a lion wouldn't come close to something smelling as strange as a Land Rover, and secondly, he couldn't get through these windows.'

He wasn't laughing at her, and she was grateful for that.

'He could try,' she insisted. 'He could get his paw through, anyway.'

'We'll close the windows, if you like,' he suggested.

But she felt better now, close to him. Very close to him, she realised, and her heart thudded unevenly against her ribs.

'I'm all right now,' she whispered, not quite steadily. 'I'll go back now.'

'That's probably a good idea,' Rob agreed, and she realised, with wonder, that his voice was unsteady too.

But neither of them moved, and soon his lips found hers. Gently at first, and then not at all gently, and his arms drew her closer to him, and all she wanted was to belong to him completely.

With shocking suddenness, he released her.

Bewildered, shaken, she would have gone back into his arms, her mouth seeking his, but he held her from him.

'Girl dear,' he said unevenly, 'I don't want you to be doing anything you'll regret later. So I think you'd better move away, if you don't mind.'

But I do mind, Julie thought, I want to stay in your arms, Rob, I want you to make love to me.

She thought, afterwards, that if she had said it at that moment he would have held her, and they would have stayed together through the warm, still night.

But she didn't say it.

With a small sigh she rolled away from him, as far away as possible in the small space, and lay still, staring into the darkness.

'Julie,' Rob said softly.

In the darkness, his hand found hers and held it for a moment.

'Goodnight,' he said.

'Goodnight, Rob,' she replied, and before his hand left hers all her resentment had gone. He was right, of course he was right. Now that she could think clearly, it was obvious that she hadn't really known what she was doing. She was hurt and confused about David—lonely—and Rob was there, an attractive man who had made it clear that he found her attractive too. So she probably would have regretted it in the morning.

And, she thought with honesty, Rob might have regretted it too. After all, he had made it all too clear that he didn't want any committed relationship, and he might have been afraid that this was what he was letting himself in for.

And there was something else too, she thought—a little sleepily, now. She had already seen that Rob would stop at nothing to try to bring Sarah and David together, to try to give Timothy and Clare back their mother and father together. Maybe he would even feel it was a good idea to—to take her thoughts and her attention from David.

And yet he was the one who had drawn back. Her cheeks were warm as she admitted to herself that she certainly would not have been able to.

Her confused, bewildering thoughts whirled round. And then, slowly, weariness won, and she fell asleep.

The clear early morning sun shining in on her face woke her. She sat up, looking for Rob.

He was outside, already clearing some of the smaller rocks away.

'Hi,' he said cheerfully, as she climbed out, rubbing her eyes. 'I think we're going to be able to creep round here, if we can clear a few more. Do you want to work first and eat afterwards, or the other way?'

Remembering the night before, she was grateful for his brisk and matter-of-fact approach.

'Work first, while it's cool,' she told him.

An hour later, tired and with every muscle aching, she watched, her heart in her mouth, as Rob eased the big vehicle, inch by inch, over the path they had cleared. Only a four-wheel-drive could have done it, and there was one moment when it seemed to Julie that the wheels on the side of the deep drop were almost over the edge. And then, unbelievably, with a final easing of the steer-ing-wheel, Rob and the Land Rover were on the other side, where the road was clear.

Julie scrambled over to join him.

'I think we've earned out breakfast,' Rob said, and she saw now that he was white under his suntan, and realised that he had been much more nervous than he had let her see.

They ate the rest of the sandwiches and gratefully finished the coffee.

'How much further?' Julie asked, when she had packed away the flask again.

'An hour—maybe a little longer,' Rob told her.

When the circle of round thatched huts was in sight, he stopped, so that she could change into her uniform.

'How do I look?' she asked him.

'Sure and Florence Nightingale herself would be proud of you,' he assured her. He took out his handkerchief then, and very gently cleaned her face, as if she were a small child. 'The best we can manage,' he said, and smiled down at her. 'I wouldn't say your face is clean, but it's less dirty than it was!'

The people at the village didn't seem to think it strange that they had arrived today instead of yesterday, but when Rob explained about the landslide some of the men got on their small sturdy ponies and went off to clear what they could, so that they would have no trouble returning to the hospital.

There were, as Rob had said, a number of dressings to change, and some stitching to be done. In all her years of nursing Julie had never had to work under conditions such as these. There was a huge black pot set on the fire, with boiling water in it, and this was all they had to sterilise any instrument that had to be used again. She handed Rob instruments, and bandaged for him, and although they worked under the shade of a huge camphor tree it became very hot. But there were so many people to see before they moved on to the next settlement.

Through the long hot day they worked side by side—except that, in each of the three settlements, Julie took half an hour to gather the women together, to talk to them about birth control, about the need for healthy eating, for no smoking, during pregnancy, about how important it was for them to come to the hospital to have regular check-ups.

'But I do see now,' she admitted to Rob, 'that it's asking a lot of them to come all that way, specially if the pregnancy is normal. What we need is for me to come to them more regularly.'

He glanced down at her. 'And what we need for that,' he pointed out, 'is more staff, so that you can leave the hospital more easily—another Land Rover. And I doubt if any of that is possible.'

'So what do we do?' Julie asked him.

His jaw was a hard line. 'We do the best we damned well can,' he said shortly. Then he smiled. 'Sorry, Julie. Been a long day, hasn't it?'

It has, Julie thought, and yet through it all Rob had worked cheerfully and professionally, talking to his patients, telling them what they had to do, never impatient with her, never asking more than she could give.

Rob Kennedy, you're quite a doctor, she said to him silently. She wished she had the courage to say it out loud—but perhaps, after the emotion of last night, it was better not to.

★   ★   ★

Back at the hospital the next day, the brief interlude away might almost not have happened, Julie found herself thinking.

Almost.

But just when this feeling was strongest, she would find her face warm with colour when she remembered how she had felt in Rob's arms. And quickly, rationally, she would remind herself of the reasons why it had happened, the reasons she had been so vulnerable. And, of course, that was the only sensible way to look at it.

Rather to her own surprise, she had become accustomed to seeing Sarah Shaw around the hospital. Sometimes the two young women happened to be alone in the dining-room, for now that they had the security of their mother's presence, Timothy and Clare played outside contentedly.

Julie found Sarah surprisingly easy to talk to. A little cautiously at first, she asked Sarah about her nursing days, and soon they found themselves swapping stories and experiences.

'But you must have been at Groote Schuur when David was there!' Sarah exclaimed, as they worked out whether Julie had known a girl Sarah had trained with. 'Did you know each other?'

Julie's heart turned over. 'Yes—yes, we did,' she replied, and hoped her voice was steady.

'David didn't mention that,' Sarah said, obviously surprised.

'Mummy, look at me, I'm up the big tree!' Clare's voice reached them through the open window.

'My goodness, you're high!' Julie said, relieved to be able to turn away to go to the window.

'Thank you,' Clare replied composedly, and Julie's and Sarah's eyes met in shared and suppressed laughter.

'You must have been worried about her,' Julie

remarked, as they sat down again and Sarah refilled their coffee-cups.

'Well, of course I was,' Sarah said carefully, after a moment. 'When David phoned, I was frantic. So I phoned Rob, and I wasn't so worried, after that. Oh, I knew she wasn't well, and Rob was very definite that he thought I should come, but——' And then, her voice bright and clear, 'Anyway, she's certainly fine now.'

Julie remembered that moment of silent communication between Rob and Sarah when she had arrived, and wondered what Rob had told David's wife. Certainly nothing about her, she was sure of that, for Sarah's manner to her was open and friendly.

David himself, since Sarah arrived, had behaved exactly as a senior doctor should towards a senior sister in a small hospital. Friendly, courteous, and pleasant.

And as if we were strangers, and always had been, Julie found herself thinking bleakly sometimes. And yet—did she want it to be any different?

'The party should be fun tonight,' said Sarah, as she took the empty coffee-cups to the serving hatch. 'Meg would rather we could have had it up at the mission station, but if we have it here pretty well everyone can come, and you're all on the spot if there's any emergency.'

Meg had decided to have a party for Sarah, and it was to be held in the dining-room. The nurses had drawn lots for hour-long spells on duty, and Julie was glad her spell was right at the beginning. When Elsa Braun came over to relieve her, she slipped back to her room and changed quickly, hesitating only for a moment before she slipped on a soft sea-green dress with shoestring straps. It was, she knew, not really suitable for this casual evening, but the sea-green of the dress made her eyes more green than grey, and somehow brought out the slight reddish tinge in her brown hair. And the golden glow of her suntanned shoulders made her quick sunbathing trips down to the river worthwhile.

Across the dusty courtyard the sound of voices and laughter reached her, and when she opened the door little Clare ran to meet her.

'You're just in time to see me do my dance,' she said. 'Oh, Julie, you do look pretty—like a fairy princess!'

'Thank you, Clare,' Julie replied, taking the small brown hand held out to her. 'You look like a princess yourself.'

'Yes, that's what I thought when I looked in Mummy's big mirror,' Clare agreed. She pulled Julie towards Rob. 'Sit here,' she commanded, 'and you'll see me prop'ly.'

'It's the best seat in the house,' Rob told her, and reached out a hand and drew Julie down beside him.

She had hardly seen him since they returned from the trip to the distant settlements, and for a moment, as she felt his eyes resting on her face, as she saw his open admiration, she wished she had resisted the temptation to wear the dress.

'Been doing some sunbathing down at the waterfall?' he asked, laughter in his dark blue eyes. 'I'm sorry I missed that.'

'My music, please, Daddy,' Clare called imperiously, and David put the 'Dance of the Little Cygnets' on the tape recorder.

With a complete lack of self-consciousness, the little girl began to dance, and Julie thought once again that, young as Clare was, there was surely a promise of real talent in her movements.

When she had finished, and made a deep, slightly unsteady curtsy, everyone in the room applauded.

'You missed seeing me doing karate,' Timothy told Julie.

'I'm sorry about that,' Julie said, meaning it. 'Did you do it all by yourself?'

'No, Rob helped me,' Timothy explained. 'I taught him what to do.'

'And very useful I'll be finding it, when I go back out into the wicked world,' Rob said gravely.

Meg and Steve came over then, bringing with them a couple in their early forties.

'This is Daniel and Elizabeth Ndlovu,' Meg said, introducing them. 'Thanks to your father's Rotary Club, Julie, they're off next week to spend some time at the Valley Trust.'

Julie shook hands with the man and the woman, and then, haltingly, wished them well in their own language.

'Thank you, Sister Norton,' Daniel Ndlovu said. 'Who is teaching you to speak our language?'

'Patience is trying to teach me a few words,' Julie told him. 'Do you know our Patience?'

For a moment the African man's and woman's eyes met.

'We have known Patience for many years,' Elizabeth said. 'And my sister is Simon's mother.'

Rob Kennedy leaned forward. 'Then you know that things are difficult for Patience?' he asked urgently. 'You know that Simon—and, perhaps even more, Simon's family—don't like the idea of Patience training to be a nurse? Look, would you come with me, to speak to Simon and his parents?'

'But we're going away,' Daniel said.

'We'll go tomorrow, or the next day,' Rob told him. 'Look, Daniel, Elizabeth, this girl is a born nurse. It would be tragic if she didn't train. But more than that, this is a chance for Patience to do what you're doing—to go out and learn something, and to come back and use that learning, that training, for the benefit of her people. Will you help me, and help Patience?'

This time Daniel and Elizabeth didn't have to look at each other.

'Yes, Dr Kennedy, we will help,' Daniel said firmly.

When they had gone, Rob turned to Julie. 'For the first time,' he said, his lean brown face alight, 'I do feel I have a chance of helping Patience. That was a bit of luck, meeting just the right people.'

Looking at him, listening to him, Julie thought, as she had thought before, that he was a strange and disturbing man, Dr Rob Kennedy. Sometimes he was light-hearted, amusing, seeming to take nothing seriously. But she knew very well that he was a dedicated doctor, and she knew now that as well as that he was a man who took other people's problems seriously. Other countries' problems.

For a moment she had a strange thought.

If it had been David she had asked to help Patience, would he have done as much, would he have cared as much?

But she knew the answer, knew it deep in her heart.

'Almost time for you to sing now, Rob,' said Meg, coming back to them. 'I just want to peep in on my babies first.'

'I want to see them too,' Julie said, getting to her feet.

She followed Meg across to the small room on the other side of the passage, where there were a few children and babies sleeping. In the dim light, as Meg bent over her own two—Faith curled up on a mattress on the floor, and baby Robin in his carrycot—Julie could see little Mark Wilson, only just fitting into his carrycot now, and two small black children fast asleep beside Faith, the little boy with his thumb in his mouth. The blanket had come off them, and she knelt down and covered them up again, gently, so as not to disturb the sleeping children.

As she straightened, she saw Rob standing in the doorway, watching her, and there was something strange and disturbing in his eyes, in the stillness of his face.

But a moment later she told herself she had imagined it, as he walked back with Meg and her, an arm around each of them, lightly, casually.

He picked up his guitar when they went into the crowded room, sat down, and began to play it.

Julie hadn't known what to expect, but now, as she sat across the room looking at his bent dark head, and listening to him sing—his voice, she thought, like brown velvet, deep and smooth—unselfconscious, like little Clare with her dancing, absorbed in the music, in the words, she thought that this was yet another unknown aspect to this man.

He was singing 'Galway Bay', and as he sang his voice became even more Irish than usual, and Julie listened, entranced, to the familiar words, for it was one of her mother's favourites.

Then, on the last line, he raised his head, and across the room his deep blue eyes held hers. And it seemed to Julie, as she listened to him sing of watching the sun go down on Galway Bay, that he was telling her that he wanted to do that, with her beside him. And that is nothing but foolish and fanciful, Julie told herself firmly.

For what in all the world gave her the right to think that Rob Kennedy would think she was as—special as all that?

And anyway, she had got all her confusing feelings for the Irish doctor neatly sorted out, she understood why she had felt the way she did, and there was absolutely no reason to let a sentimental Irish song make her feel any differently.

He was singing 'I'll Take You Home Again, Kathleen' now, and when he had finished that, and would have got up, his audience wouldn't allow him to. But Julie was extremely relieved when, at the end of 'Danny Boy', he gave in to Timothy's pleas and sang 'Paddy McGinty's Goat'.

Everyone loved it, and he sang it very well, but the mood and the spell were broken, and she was glad of that.

Soon after that, the people from the mission station went back up the hill, and the party broke up. Little Clare was almost asleep, and Julie, putting empty cups on a tray, saw David bend down and lift her up.

'I'll carry her to the cottage,' he said to Sarah, and smiled down at her.

Julie's hands were still. This was the first moment of real closeness she had seen between David and Sarah. And as they went out, with Timothy, tired too, but unwilling to admit it, holding Sarah's hand, and Clare asleep now in her father's arms, Julie thought, with complete clarity, That's how they should be.

And she knew that if there was anything within her power that she could do to help them to remain that way, she would do it.

'You're almost asleep too,' said Rob, coming up behind her. 'We've done enough clearing, let's call it a day. Or maybe a night.'

He had seen her watching David and his wife and his children, she knew that. As they walked across the moonlit courtyard together, she wanted to tell him how she had felt, she wanted him to understand that she could never do anything to come between them, to jeopardise their chances of putting their differences right. But the words were not easy to find, and she was tired, so she thought she would tell him some other time.

And that was something she was to regret.

'Goodnight, Julie,' Rob murmured, when they reached the door to the women's rooms.

His lips brushed her cheek, lingered for a moment, and then found her mouth. It was a long kiss, long and slow and very satisfactory, Julie thought, dazed, when they drew apart.

She hadn't meant it to happen, but she certainly didn't regret it, and when she left Rob and went into her room she was humming the sweet and plaintive tune of 'Danny Boy'.

Knowing she was on duty at seven the next morning, she got ready for bed quickly, leaving her sea-green dress over the back of the chair. Tomorrow, she thought sleepily, I'll tidy everything.

She seemed to have only just fallen asleep when she woke, her heart thudding, to hear someone knocking at her door and saying her name.

To her surprise it was Monika Jansen, and even in the dim light from the corridor Julie could see that she looked dreadful.

'Monika—what on earth is wrong?' she asked, helping the German nurse into her room, and putting on the light.

'I would not have bothered you,' Monika said, with difficulty, 'but Elsa is not there, she is on the ward, and I could not wake Sister Nguli.'

Her face was grey, and her forehead damp, Julie saw, shocked.

'I—do not feel well,' she said, and closed her eyes.

Julie lifted her wrist. Her pulse was racing, and she was already in shock.

'Where do you have pain, Monika?' she asked, keeping her voice steady.

'Here,' the German nurse said, and she put her hand

to her stomach. 'For a few days now it is painful, and I think it is something I have eaten, but—now, I do not think it can be.'

There was no time to be wasted, Julie knew that. 'Lie down on my bed, Monika,' she said, and put her duvet over the girl. 'I'm going to get Dr Kennedy.'

'Perhaps I feel better in the morning,' Monika protested.

Julie shook her head. 'Not without finding out what the trouble is,' she said decisively. 'I won't be long.'

She ran across the silent courtyard, pulling on her dressing-gown as she went. It seemed to her an age before Rob responded to her urgent knocking, and opened the door.

'What is it?' he demanded sharply.

'Monika's ill,' she told him. 'She's in shock, her pulse is racing, and she has abdominal pain.'

She hadn't even finished speaking before he was pulling jeans on over the shorts that were all he was wearing, and lifted a cotton T-shirt from the chair, as they hurried out, and his medical bag.

'I am sorry to disturb you,' Monika said, when they reached Julie's room. 'I would have waited, but Julie said——'

'Julie was quite right,' Rob interrupted her. 'Now, just lie still, and relax as much as you can, while I find out what the trouble is.'

Swiftly, expertly, he examined her, and the few questions he asked confirmed what Julie was already thinking.

'You probably suspected appendicitis yourself,' he said at last, to Monika. 'And I'm sure Julie did. I'm going to give you something to make you feel more comfortable, Monika, but we'll have to deal with this right away.'

A moment later, with Monika's eyes already becoming heavy, he turned to Julie.

'Wake Patience,' he said crisply, 'and tell her to go and get David—I need him for the anaesthetic. Will you assist? I'd rather have you than Elsa, quite frankly, or Agnes.'

'Of course,' Julie replied.

Rob glanced down at the woman on the bed. She was almost unconscious now. 'Leave her here while you dress, then we'll get a trolley and take her over.'

It was only twenty minutes later, Julie realised, that they were in the theatre, David checking the anaesthetic and Rob preparing to operate, while she prepared the instruments.

'You're sure, I suppose?' David asked abruptly.

'Yes, I'm sure,' Rob replied, without turning round from the sink where he was scrubbing up. 'Diffuse tenderness around the umbilicus and the midepigastrium, and I got Rovsing's Sign by palpating the lower left quadrant, and she felt pain in the right lower quadrant. There was also extreme muscular rigidity, and right hip flexing suggesting inflammation of the psoas muscle. Do you still query my diagnosis?'

Julie took the packet of surgical gloves and walked quickly across the theatre to where Rob was waiting, his hands raised.

There was nothing she could do or say that wouldn't be interfering. But the latent hostility between the two doctors was becoming more and more disturbing, and not, she knew, the best atmosphere for the operation on Monika.

'Your gloves, Dr Kennedy,' she said.

Above their masks, his eyes met hers, and with a wave of relief she saw the tightness of his face relax.

'Sorry, David,' he said, before the other man could reply. 'I know it's always a tricky diagnosis, but yes, I am sure. Now, what do you think about the incision? McBurney or Rockey-Davis?'

'I'd go for the Rockey-Davis, myself,' David replied, after a moment. 'I prefer that transverse cut. Especially if you think the appendix is likely to rupture.'

'I think we're going to be just in time,' Rob said. 'Is her breathing stable? Fine, I'll go ahead.'

He took the sterilised scalpel from Julie, and made the first incision, his hand sure and steady. And as the operation progressed Julie saw that he hadn't forgotten her lack of recent theatre experience, for he gave her clear instructions as to the instruments he needed.

But other than his instructions, and a murmured exchange between the two doctors as to Monika's condition, the small operating theatre was silent. It was only when Rob removed the appendix that he said, his voice startlingly loud, 'As I thought, just in time. Another half-hour and we could have been in trouble.'

He began to work on the inside stitches now, and because he had been able to remove the diseased appendix before it ruptured this was a straightforward job.

'Fowler's position,' he said to Julie as he finished, and threw down his gloves, just missing the waste-bin. 'But I don't expect any complications, thanks to you acting quickly.' At the door, he turned. 'Thanks, David,' he said. 'Sorry to have disturbed your night's sleep.'

There was no recovery-room in the small hospital, so Julie sat with Monika in the operating theatre until she came out of the anaesthetic.

'I bring you tea, Julie,' Elsa Braun said breathlessly, coming in after the two doctors had left. 'How is Monika?'

'She's going to be fine,' Julie told her. 'Dr Kennedy removed the appendix before it ruptured, so her recovery should be straightforward. You have enough to do in the ward, I'll stay with her until we can take her through.'

A little later she saw her patient's eyelids flicker.

'It's all over, Monika,' she said reassuringly. 'Your appendix is gone, and you'll feel much better. Don't try to stay awake.'

'But I want to thank you,' Monika told her, with difficulty. 'You did the right thing for me, and—I know it would have been much worse if we had waited.'

Julie patted her hand. 'I'm glad you came to me, Monika,' she said, meaning it.

And when she left her patient in the women's side of the general ward an hour later, in Elsa's care, she thought that perhaps things would be better between Monika and her now, perhaps the breach that she had never really understood might begin to be healed.

'They're already a week late for school,' Sarah Shaw remarked, looking at the two children playing under the waterfall in the river.

It was a week after the party, and Monika Jansen's dramatic appendectomy, and in that time Julie had often found Sarah—and the children—waiting for her any time she was off duty.

Today, when she had the whole day off, Sarah had suggested they might bring a picnic down to the river. Even early in the morning it was hot, and this shaded place was delightfully cool, with the sound of the water-fall, and the deep pool at its base.

'There's certainly nothing wrong with Clare now,' Julie commented. And then, 'Does it matter for them, missing school?'

Sarah hesitated. 'I suppose it does,' she said after a moment. 'Specially for Timothy. But it seemed more important for them, for all of us, to stay on here. There were things that had to be sorted out.' Her clear blue eyes met Julie's. 'I'm sure you heard when you came that David and I were separated,' she said quietly.

'Yes, I did,' Julie replied, for Sarah's honesty demanded honesty in return.

'It seemed the only thing to do,' Sarah went on, her voice low, her eyes, unseeing, on the sunlight shining through the trees on to the pool. 'Things weren't working—they hadn't been for some time. David—can be very demanding. But, at the same time, he isn't very supportive as a husband and a father.'

She smiled, but it was a sad little smile that didn't reach her eyes.

'In some ways, he's never grown up. And there were other things too. David always has to have an adoring woman around him. In the early years of our marriage, it was enough for him to have me in that role. But I think, Julie, that after the children came I did some growing up myself, I became more involved with them, and—well, David had to look beyond our marriage. Or he felt he had to.'

Without asking Sarah, Julie refilled their mugs with the coffee that was left in the flask, and handed one to this girl who, she realised with a shock, she had come to look on as a friend.

'I don't think he was ever unfaithful to me,' Sarah went on, and Julie could see that she needed to talk about this. 'But suddenly I'd had enough. I knew we couldn't go on like that, and I knew he had to see that. So I told him I wanted a separation. It seemed the only way of saving our marriage, strangely enough. Maybe I wasn't seeing too clearly, but I thought—I thought it would bring him to his senses, he would realise that he couldn't risk losing us, the children and me.'

At the other side of the pool, Clare—so very like her

father, Julie thought again—splashed her brother and laughed as he splashed her in return, her clear, childish laughter ringing in the quietness of the river pool. How could David risk breaking up his family? Julie found herself thinking.

'But it rather backfired on me,' Sarah said then. 'David went all huffy, and took this job in the mission hospital, and there we were miles apart. I came here with the children a couple of times. And I could see, the last time, that he was beginning to miss us. But, at the same time, still the same old David—Monika Jansen would lie down and let him walk over her, and I think so would Elsa.'

And that, Julie remembered, was one of the reasons Rob had given her for Monika resenting her, the fact that she and David had once known each other.

Sarah went on to tell her that she and Rob had become friendly, and that this had helped her, in these visits. She hadn't ever, she said, been able to talk as freely to him as she had now to Julie, but she knew he had understood. And that was why she had relied on Rob's judgement and come here now.

'For some reason,' she said slowly, 'Rob seemed to feel it was important for me to be here. I'm not sure why, but I knew I had to come.' She shrugged. 'Maybe he just felt it was the right time, that David needed a push.'

'Rob certainly can have that sort of feeling,' Julie agreed. Impulsively, she put her hand over Sarah's. 'I'm very glad you did come, Sarah. And——' she hesitated '—do you think it's going to work out for you and David?'

It was a moment before Sarah replied. 'I think it is,' she said at last, carefully. 'Maybe that's because I want it so much.' She smiled, with difficulty. 'Strange as it seems, Julie, after all I've been saying I love David very much. I think I've always been fairly clear-sighted about him, but I've always loved him.'

She began to pack the picnic things back into the basket. 'Even before we were married, there was someone,' she said, her back to Julie. 'When he was in Cape Town. I knew, because I always did know, but I knew too that he wouldn't let anything come in the way of marrying me, and having my father help him to get the position he wanted in the hospital. I know my David.'

Yes, I think you do, Julie thought bleakly. 'He's very lucky that you still love him, Sarah,' she said evenly.

Sarah turned round. 'That's one way to look at it, I suppose,' she agreed. 'But the other side of the picture is that I'm not just making the best of things—love is a funny thing, you can't weigh up this and measure out that, you—just love someone. Like I love David. And I think that maybe, just maybe, he's been doing some growing up while he's been here, and maybe now we can work things out.'

'I certainly hope so,' Julie said, not quite steadily, as she lifted up the basket, and Sarah took the children's towels and clothes.

And so, Julie thought that night, sitting at her open window to enjoy the coolness of the night air, I never was as important to David as he was to me. Neither ten years ago, nor now. All he was doing now was using me as balm for his injured pride.

It was painful, and it hurt, facing up to the truth, but she had to do it. It was like lancing a boil and letting the poison out.

She hadn't spent the last ten years thinking about David, she knew that, but at the same time she had never forgotten him. Although she could see now that the David she had remembered—the David she thought she had found again when she came here—had never really existed. The only person who really knew David through and through, and accepted him, was Sarah. She always had.

She went to bed then, and rather to her own surprise slept deep and soundlessly, waking to find Monika Jansen bringing her a cup of tea. The German nurse had been out of hospital care for a day or two now, although she wasn't to start work for another week. But she had recovered quickly from her operation, and Julie, gratefully accepting the tea, commented on this.

'I am strong like horse,' Monika told her.

'Even so, you shouldn't be bringing me tea,' Julie protested. 'You should be staying in bed longer.'

Monika shrugged. 'I go back to bed now,' she said. 'And you have done much for me, now I can do this one small thing for you.'

'Oh, Monika,' Julie said, embarrassed, 'I only did what any nurse would do—I'm just glad you came to me.'

'You could have send me away, tell me to take aspirin,' Monika insisted.

In some ways, Julie thought ruefully, Monika's hostility was easier to handle than this! She thanked the German nurse again for the tea, though, and said she'd have to hurry and bath now.

Rob was to be away, she knew, making a mobile clinic visit to a nearby settlement. So it would be David who would come on ward rounds. She hadn't seen him at all since Sarah had talked to her yesterday, for he and Sarah and the children had had their evening meal at the cottage.

She found herself hoping, as she completed the charts for the three patients in the maternity ward, that David would decide to go back to Durban, back to the life that, she couldn't help feeling, was more suited to him than working here in the mission hospital. Although Rob had controlled himself that night in the theatre, Julie felt that there would always be antagonism between the two doctors, their relationship would never be smooth.

And although it might not be easy, finding a doctor to replace David here, she was certain it would be better for everyone if David was to go.

And perhaps it was because she had had these thoughts, that they were very much in her mind, that she wasn't surprised when David, accepting a cup of tea from Patience when he had finished his ward round, waited until the young girl had gone back to the ward, then said, a little awkwardly,

'I wanted to tell you, Julie—Sarah and I were talking last night. It isn't easy for her, being on her own with the children. I don't plan on leaving the hospital in the lurch here, but as soon as the committee can organise a replacement I want to leave.'

'I'm so glad to hear that, David,' Julie told him, and she could see that the warmth of her reply had taken him by surprise. 'I'm sure you've made the right decision.'

He turned away. 'It wasn't an easy decision, Julie,' he said, his voice low. 'You know things haven't been right between Sarah and me, and since you came here, since you brought so many memories back to me, it's been—very difficult.'

The noble renunciation, Julie thought, and for the first time in her relationship with this man she felt laughter bubbling up inside. And, with the laughter, a glorious sense of freedom.

'Well, now that you've decided,' she said briskly, 'I do hope you can go soon, and start making up for the time you've wasted as a family.'

He was taken aback. 'I hope you'll be all right, Julie,' he said, recovering.

'I'll be just fine,' she assured him. She held out her hand to him. 'I do hope you can make things work out, David.'

He took her hand between both of his. 'I hope so, Julie. And—I want you to know——'

What he wanted her to know, she was not to find out. There was a sound from the doorway, and they both turned round.

Rob stood there. His dark brows were drawn together, and his eyes were cold. He was, Julie saw, angry—very angry.

CHAPTER TWELVE

THERE was no reason to feel guilty, but Julie was all too conscious of a warm flood of colour in her cheeks as David released her hand.

'I thought you were away at Bulankulu,' David said.

'I came back unexpectedly,' Rob replied curtly. 'That ulcer of old Matthew Mboku's—it's perforated. I brought him back, I've set up a drip, and I think he's stabilised, but he's lost a lot of blood. I'm going to ask the hospital in Umtata to send the helicopter for him— he needs surgery immediately.' His blue eyes were very dark. 'That's what I came to talk to you about,' he said coolly. 'If we both give authorisation, it can speed things up. Elsa said you were doing rounds here. I'm—sorry to interrupt you.'

It was unforgivable, Julie knew that, to break in, but she had to.

'Dr Shaw has finished,' she said. 'Thank you, Dr Shaw. I'll let you know how Mrs Tyabule responds to the treatment.'

For a moment she thought Rob was going to say something else, then, with a curt nod, he turned and strode across the courtyard. David shrugged, and followed him.

Julie wished then that she had spoken to Rob, told him how she felt, told him that now, at last, she was completely free from the past, free from the final tie with the man she had been in love with all those years ago. If she had, he wouldn't have misunderstood what he had seen now.

But she hadn't told him, and he had misunderstood. It was all too obvious that he had thought she was still trying to hold on to David.

Resolutely, Julie put these disturbing thoughts out of her mind and got back to work. One of the newly delivered mothers had bad varicose veins, and there was a danger of venous thrombosis, so Julie had raised the foot of the bed.

'And we want you moving as much as possible, Mrs Tyabule,' she said, unobtrusively checking her patient's legs, as she adjusted the height of the bricks underneath. 'Even when you're lying, move your ankles, wiggle your toes. And Patience will help you to walk up and down the ward in a little while.'

'And if all this does not work, Sister Norton?' Patience asked her when they were back in the duty-room.

'Then we'll try low-dosage subcutaneous heparin,' Julie told her. 'Five thousand units eight-hourly. But her veins aren't too bad, we're hoping this conservative treatment works.'

She and Patience were busy for the rest of the day, with two more admissions, one of them delivering almost immediately. The helicopter arrived in the early afternoon, and Elsa Braun told Julie that the old man had been taken to hospital for surgery, and his condition when he was taken away was very much improved.

'It was very fortunate that Dr Kennedy arrived at the village soon after the old man became ill, was it not?' Elsa said earnestly that night.

'Very fortunate,' Julie agreed, and of course it was, for the old man, and she was glad that Rob's intervention had probably saved his life. But the timing had not been at all fortunate for her.

She tried to explain to Rob.

When he came into the dining-room that night, she

left her place and went up to him. 'Rob,' she said, her voice low, 'I know you must think——'

'I doubt if what I think is of any real importance to you, Julie,' he interrupted her. 'If you'll excuse me, I'm in a hurry.'

And, very pointedly, he took his plate and went to sit at the far end of the table, beside Agnes Nguli.

Julie, her cheeks flaming, her head high, went back to her own place.

All right, Dr Kennedy, she told herself defiantly, be like that! Don't bother to find out whether your interpretation of things is correct, just—just think what you want to, and see if I care!

She did care, though, she had to admit, as the days passed, and Rob's distant and cool politeness continued. But she wasn't prepared to lay herself open to another snub.

Not even to thank him for what he had done for Patience.

The young African girl came into the maternity ward a few days later, her feet flying, her eyes glowing.

'Oh, Julie, I am sorry to be late,' she said breathlessly, 'but I have been talking to Dr Kennedy, and—Julie, everything is all right, he has talked to Simon, and he has talked to Simon's father, and his mother, and he has made them see that we are young, Simon and I, and there are many years before Simon will be headman, and he will be a better headman if he can——'

Laughing, Julie put her hand on the girl's arm. 'Take your time, Patience, and tell me what's going to happen.'

Obediently, Patience took a deep breath, and slowed down. 'Simon's father agrees,' she said carefully, 'that it will be good that I train as a nurse, and then I can help to look after our people. And Dr Kennedy said to him, surely it would be good for Simon to train in something too, so Simon is to go to the college where they will teach him about cattle, and farming. We will see each other, and we will be promised to each other, and when I am a good nurse, and Simon is a good farmer, we will be married.'

'Patience, I'm so happy for you,' Julie said, and she hugged the girl. 'That really is the best answer of all.'

'And it is all thanks to Dr Kennedy,' Patience assured her. 'I am so grateful that you thought of asking him to help me, Julie.'

I should thank him, Julie thought, but the sight of the cool remoteness of the Irish doctor's face, the polite distance any time he had to speak to her, stopped her. On his ward rounds, he was completely professional, and so distant that she could hardly believe he was the same man who had held her in his arms, who had teased her, made her laugh, made her——

Made her miss his—friendship, his closeness—so much that it hurt unbearably. Sometimes she thought she would have liked to talk to Sarah about it, but because of David's part in it she could not do that.

'Is it not wonderful that Rob has solved the problems for Patience?' Sister Nguli said to her when they were the only two left after dinner one night.

'Yes—yes, it is wonderful,' Julie agreed brightly. Too brightly, she knew, for the African woman's eyes rested on her face, questioning.

'I think you have quarrelled, you and Rob,' Agnes Nguli said gently.

Julie nodded. 'Yes, we have,' she replied, her voice low.

The older woman waited, saying nothing.

'He's angry with me because he misunderstood something he saw,' Julie went on, with difficulty.

'Then you must tell him that he was wrong, you must explain to him,' the sister told her.

Julie tried to smile. 'It isn't as easy as that,' she said, her voice low. 'He's made up his mind, and—and I can't go on trying to make him see he was wrong.'

'Why not?' Agnes queried.

Julie looked at her. 'Well—I have some pride,' she said defensively.

The older woman shrugged. 'How important is it to you, Julie, that Rob should understand?'

Julie looked down at her hands, brown from the sun, clasped together. 'Very important,' she admitted.

Agnes patted her shoulder. 'Then you go and speak to him,' she advised cheerfully. 'Go right now—he is in his room, and I think he is as unhappy as you are, Julie.'

Somehow Julie found herself across the courtyard, and outside the wing where the men's rooms were. There was a light in Rob's room, and the window was open.

She went closer to it.

'Rob,' she said quietly. And then, more loudly, 'Rob, I want to talk to you.'

His dark head, rumpled, as if he had been lying on his bed, appeared at the window.

'Why?' he asked uncompromisingly.

'Because this is ridiculous, you misunderstood what you saw, and you won't let me explain,' Julie said, looking up at him.

'I didn't misunderstand,' Rob said flatly. 'I understood all too well. In spite of anything you'd said to me, there you were, with David Shaw cosily holding your hand, and never mind his wife, never mind his children, you've got him back and that's all you care for.'

Julie's temper, which had been reaching simmering-point, boiled over. 'Rob Kennedy,' she said very loudly, 'you are the most stubborn, obnoxious man I've ever met, and I don't know why it bothers me to have you thinking something that isn't true, but it does. Now, are you coming out, or do I have to come in?'

There was a long silence.

'I'll come out,' Rob said, obviously taken aback.

A moment later he was beside her.

Without waiting to see if he would follow, Julie walked briskly down the path to the river, until she was round the corner and out of sight of the hospital.

'All right, then,' Rob said cautiously, 'go ahead.'

Julie took a deep breath. 'David had just told me he was going to resign, and go back to Durban, back to Sarah and the children,' she said, her voice clear. 'I told him I was glad to hear it, and I wished him well.'

In the moonlight she could see that Rob's dark blue eyes were just a little less remote.

'It didn't look quite like that,' he said, after a moment.

'No, perhaps not,' Julie admitted. She hesitated and then said, a little awkwardly, that David had taken her hand in both of his.

'But it didn't mean anything,' she said steadily. 'Certainly not to me, and I'm sure not to him either.'

There was no need for her to feel any loyalty to David, and she told Rob now what she should have told him before, about her talk with Sarah, about her realisation that the David Shaw she had known and remembered for all these years had never existed.

'Did that hurt, finding that out?' Rob asked.

He had somehow moved closer to her, but it was more than a physical closeness, she knew with a deep relief. The remoteness between them had gone.

'A little,' she admitted. 'But—I feel free now.'

'I'm very glad of that,' Rob said, not quite steadily.

He put his arms around her and held her close to him,

and that was what she needed, what she wanted, at that moment.

'I have an idea,' he said, 'and it's a great idea, girl dear.'

Her heart lifted, for this was the old Rob, warm laughter in his voice, his arms around her, keeping her close to him.

'What's your great idea?' she asked him.

'Before David goes, and makes it impossible for me to get away, we will have a few days off, just you and me, Julie.' He put one hand over her mouth, stilling her protests. 'I'm sure you're due a weekend off, and I certainly am, and with an extra day on each side we can go to the Wild Coast. Have you ever been to the Wild Coast, Julie?'

'No, I haven't, but——'

'But nothing, then, the Wild Coast it is,' Rob said sweepingly. 'I will make the arrangements, for I have a friend who is manager at one of the hotels at the mouth of the Quala River. You will love it, for it is like heaven on earth.'

They began to walk back up the path, Rob with one arm still around her.

'You extravagant Irishman,' Julie said, and she was laughing now, 'heaven on earth indeed!'

'I swear it,' Rob told her solemnly. He stopped, and looked down at her, and now he was serious again. 'And no strings attached, Julie. Just a break, at a time when I'm thinking you could be doing with it.'

Perhaps heaven on earth was something of an exaggeration, Julie thought, a few days later, as they arrived at Seacrest, but it was a glorious situation.

The Wild Coast was well named. There was a lagoon, there were cliffs, there was the river, with trees growing luxuriantly right to its mouth, there was a sandy bay, and miles and miles of unspoiled golden sand.

The hotel itself consisted of small thatched rondavels, just like the native huts, and one low building which housed the dining-room and the huge, sea-facing lounge.

'A little primitive, perhaps,' Rob said, as he carried Julie's suitcase into her rondavel for her.

Julie looked around the small room, with its bed, a wardrobe built into the curve of the room, a tiny bath-room with a shower—'Which may or may not work,' Rob told her—and the intricate thatching rising to a peak.

'I love it,' she said, with complete truth.

That night she slept soundly, waking to the sound of the sea incredibly close. It was a beautiful day, and she pulled on her bathing-costume and ran barefoot down the golden sand to the incoming tide. The water was cool, so early in the morning, but not cold, and in a moment she had run out far enough to swim.

The shore sloped gently here at the mouth of the river, and she was far out, looking back towards the group of small thatched rondavels, when she saw Rob come down to the water's edge and swim out towards her.

'I came to tell you your morning tea is waiting for you,' he said when he reached her. 'Thought I'd have to wake you up.'

Julie pushed her wet hair back from her face. 'I'll go back and drink it now,' she said. 'Race you!'

They reached the shallow water at the same time, and Rob caught her hand and pulled her to her feet, still keeping her hand in his as they walked up the beach together.

'How energetic do you feel?' he asked her later, as they were finishing breakfast.

'How energetic do you want me to feel?' Julie asked cautiously.

He leaned forward. 'Well, there's this wreck in the next bay—we could walk along, and swim out to the rocks, and have a look at it.'

This was, he told her, a coast of shipwrecks, for there were treacherous rocks outside the peaceful bays.

They set off after breakfast, walking barefoot on the golden sand, and the only person they saw, in the distance, was a solitary fisherman. When they came within sight of the rocks where the ship had been wrecked—eighty or ninety years ago, Rob said vaguely— they left their clothes and towels on the beach, and swam out. There wasn't a great deal of the ship left now, but it was still a strange feeling, to think of this ship sailing the oceans, to think of the people who had sailed on her.

'It makes me shiver to think of them all down there,' Julie said, peering down into the sea.

'Shiver if you want to,' Rob replied, 'but actually, no one drowned in this shipwreck, they all managed to get ashore before she broke up.'

'Oh,' Julie said, deflated. Then she saw the corner of his mouth twitching. 'I never know if you're serious or not,' she told him.

'Sometimes I am, and sometimes I'm not,' he told her. 'Let's get back.'

After their energetic morning, they were both content to lie in the sun in the afternoon, with the waves lapping gently beside them. Julie, almost asleep, was conscious of Rob moving beside her.

'You're going to burn if you don't have more suntan oil on,' he warned, and she felt his hand, warm and large and competent, smoothing oil into her back, over her shoulders.

'That feels nice,' she murmured drowsily. His hand,

on her shoulder, had stopped, and she opened her eyes and turned over. He was looking down at her. She couldn't see his eyes, because of his sunglasses, but he was unsmiling. And there was something about his stillness that made her heart thud unsteadily.

When he kissed her, his lips were faintly salty. Or perhaps hers were. And his body was warm from the sun, warm against hers.

Perhaps, she thought later, they both remembered at the same time that they were on the beach, in full view of anyone who might walk round the corner from the hotel. Reluctantly, they drew apart.

There was a streak of sand on Rob's face, and Julie touched it with one finger. 'You've got sand on your face,' she told him unsteadily.

He smiled down at her. 'So have you,' he said. 'I think it's the same sand.'

The next morning they took the motorboat that belonged to the hotel, and went up the river. Gradually the trees seemed to close in, until they were in a green tunnel. Rob shut down the motor, and they floated in a silent and deserted world.

'It's magic, this place,' Julie said when they turned back towards the mouth of the river again.

'I know,' Rob agreed. His eyes met hers. 'I've been here a few times—I wanted to share it with you.'

He seemed to be waiting, she thought, waiting for her to say something, perhaps to do something. But she didn't know what.

'It feels as if we've been here for ages,' she said, turning away, trailing her hand in the water.

'Yes, it does,' he agreed, and she thought she must have imagined the look of faint disappointment on his face.

They walked along beside the sea after dinner that

night, the moonlight clear enough for them to see their way. Words didn't seem to be necessary, but Rob kept her hand in his all the time. When they got back to their adjoining rondavels, he took her in his arms.

'Goodnight, girl dear,' he murmured, his lips still close to hers.

She stirred in his arms. 'Rob——' she began, not sure what she wanted to say. But he put one finger on her lips.

'Ssh, now,' he said softly. 'Will you be remembering, now, that I said no strings attached?'

But what if I want the strings attached? Julie thought a little ruefully, alone in her rondavel. What if I don't want to be kissed goodnight and left?

In fact, she thought, slowly, honestly, she didn't really know what she wanted. Somehow this place had brought a new depth to her relationship with Rob. But there were still doubts. What did she want of him, and what did he want of her? He had never said anything that told her he thought of her as anything but an attractive girl to spend his time with. And yet—if that was all, why did he draw back when he must know that it would take very little to overcome any slight resistance she might have?

And her own feelings were confusing. If—if she was beginning to fall in love with him, if this wasn't rebound, chemistry, proximity, whatever—if it was none of these things, then surely she was jumping from the frying-pan into the fire, from being in love with a married man to being in love with a man who wanted to remain footloose and fancy-free!

Reluctantly, though, she saw that it would surely have made things even more difficult, even more complicated, if she and Rob hadn't parted when they said goodnight.

But it was a strange and disturbing thought, that she was lying here in her bed, and such a short distance away

Rob was in his. Just a few steps between them. But—no strings attached, he had said.

She woke early the next morning, knowing it was their last complete day, wanting to make the most of it. Perhaps she would have an early swim, she thought, and then later they had promised themselves to walk down the coast in the other direction, towards the next river-mouth.

A knock at the door told her that her early morning tea had arrived, and she poured a cup and sat down at the open door to drink it. Just as she was deciding between more tea or that early swim, Rob came out of his rondavel.

'Did you switch on the news?' he asked her.

Startled, she put her cup down and said she hadn't.

'There's been a minor earthquake,' he told her. 'The radio reception is bad, and I missed half of it, but it seems it's very close to the hospital. They mentioned the mission station. We'd better phone, and find out what's happened.'

The only telephone was in the manager's office, but fortunately he was already up when Rob knocked on his door.

'Yes, I heard the news too,' he said, 'but I didn't catch the name of the mission station.'

He stood back while Rob dialled. Dialled, and then tried again.

'I can't get through,' he said at last. 'The lines must be down.' His eyes were very dark, and his mouth set. 'We've got to go back, Julie,' he said. 'Right away.'

CHAPTER THIRTEEN

THEY left an hour later, still unable to get any more news, and there was no radio in the Land Rover.

'We should be there in three hours,' Rob said, soon after they left. He hesitated, then added, 'Unless there are roads or bridges damaged.'

Julie wondered if Rob, like herself, was remembering the recent earthquake in California, and the horror of the freeway collapsing. But this, she reminded herself, had been described as a minor earthquake.

But how minor is minor? she couldn't help wondering. Especially when there might be people you know involved.

'I wish Sarah and the children had gone,' she said, her voice low.

Sarah was to be going in two days, she remembered. She had planned to wait until Rob and Julie got back, so that David would be free to take her and the children to Umtata.

The rest of the hospital staff, and any patients there, she thought. And the people at the mission station, the people she knew and loved. Meg and Steve, little Faith, baby Robin. The Wilsons, and baby Mark. The women who went there every day to do their weaving.

She turned away, but not quickly enough, for Rob, glancing at her, had seen that she was close to tears.

'Stop it, Julie!' he told her, quite roughly. But his hand, covering hers for a moment, wasn't at all rough, it was warm and comforting and strengthening. 'You won't do yourself any good dwelling on what we may find. Now tell me, what's in that basket that Jack Hearn insisted on giving us?'

They had had a hurried breakfast before leaving, and the manager had put a large basket into the Land Rover.

'Some rolls, he said, some cold chicken, a flask of coffee,' Julie told him. She twisted round and inspected the basket. 'And all obviously meant to be used without stopping—he knew we'd just want to keep going.'

When they stopped for petrol, they asked for news of the hospital, but the garage owner wasn't there, and the petrol attendant just nodded vigorously and said yes, he had heard that the earth had moved, but he didn't know where this had happened.

The journey to the Wild Coast had passed so quickly, Julie remembered. She had watched the changing scenery with interest, she and Rob had talked, they had laughed, and she had waited for her first sight of the sea.

But now, driving back seemed to take much longer. Neither of them felt like speaking, the sea was behind them, and they didn't know what lay ahead.

When it was lunchtime, Julie passed Rob some cold chicken and a roll, and they stopped for five minutes to drink coffee and to stretch, before the final hour's drive.

'One more bridge to go,' Rob said tightly, as they neared the final bridge before the hospital. If it was down, they could be held up long enough, unable to get across the river.

But the bridge was undamaged, and Rob drove over it, and along to the turn-off to the hospital. Julie leaned forward, hardly able to breathe, as they rounded the last bend.

And there stood the hospital, low and squat and functional, just as they had left it. Undamaged, Julie thought, with a flood of relief.

Rob touched her hand. 'Look,' he said quietly.

He pointed up the hill, to the mission station itself, and her relief changed to horror. For half of the buildings had collapsed, and where the large hall and weaving-shed had been there was only rubble.

She couldn't remember the Land Rover stopping, and she couldn't remember getting out, but she and Rob were in the courtyard, hurrying into the general ward.

Every bed was full. David was bending over one bed, adjusting a splint on a man's leg. Sarah was bandaging a child's arm, Agnes Nguli was putting a dressing on a woman's shoulder, Monika Jansen and Elsa Braun were each cleaning wounds.

Rob touched David's shoulder, and the other doctor looked round.

'Thank heavens you're here!' he exclaimed, with heartfelt relief.

He straightened up. Julie had never seen David look like this. There was a streak of grime down his cheek, his fair hair was untidy, and his eyes were red-rimmed.

'How bad is it?' Rob asked him.

'Pretty bad, at the mission station, and at the two nearest settlements,' David told him. 'We were incredibly lucky here. But it could be worse. Everyone got outside in time, and there are no fatalities. Breaks, bruises, concussion—and burns, from some of the huts collapsing, and paraffin stoves setting the thatch on fire. They're still bringing people in from the settlements.'

'Where should I start?' Rob asked.

David wiped the back of his hand over his forehead. 'When Monika and Elsa finish cleaning up see what has to be done, there might be stitching, or splinting.' He looked at Julie. 'Before you do anything, Julie, you'd better check with Patience, she's over with the mothers and babies.'

Julie hurried across to her own ward. The young African girl's face lit up with relief when she went in.

'I am so glad you are here, Sister Norton,' she said breathlessly. 'I am doing as Dr Shaw says and keeping everyone calm and not worrying, but now they have brought in Mrs Molweni—her baby is not due for a month, but the hut collapsed on her, and although she is not badly hurt she has gone into labour.'

Swiftly, expertly, Julie checked the African woman. She was indeed in labour, and strong labour too. Her arm had been cut, but Patience had cleaned it and bandaged it.

'My baby is coming too soon, Sister,' the woman said, obviously alarmed.

Julie patted her hand. 'A little sooner than we would like,' she agreed. 'But your baby is quite big already, big enough to be born, and the heartbeat is good and strong.'

She turned to Patience. 'I think she'll be another hour,' she said quietly. 'I can do a fair bit to help across there until then.' She glanced around the ward. 'When you need me, send one of the mothers over for me, don't leave Mrs Molweni alone.'

She hurried back to the general ward. Already, with Rob there to help, the line of people waiting patiently had become smaller. But she could see, coming down the hill, a small group of people carrying someone, and another man supported between two people. So there were still injured people coming in.

Out on the veranda, she could see that Meg and Helen were dealing with the people who had been bandaged or splinted, and who needed a cup of tea and some reassurance more than anything. Julie joined Sarah in dressing burns.

'Go and have some tea now,' she told them, when their

dressings were done, but the men and women just stood there, looking at her blankly.

'Shock,' Sarah said, glancing up. 'There are quite a few like that. I've heard that an earthquake can affect people this way. Take them outside, Julie—we need the space here.'

Julie led the group of men and women—silent and docile and unquestioning—out to where Meg had made a huge pot of tea.

'You'll feel much better when you have some tea,' she told them firmly. 'Now sit down, over here on the steps, and we'll see that you get some tea.'

As Helen Wilson carried mugs of hot sweet tea over, Julie joined Meg.

'Where are the children?' she asked.

'In the dining-room,' Meg said briefly. 'Timothy's in charge, with Clare helping him, and you wouldn't believe it, but the babies are actually sleeping. Fortunately they're all too young to have got too much of a fright.'

'Are you all right?' Julie asked.

Meg smiled. 'I'm fine,' she said. 'We were incredibly lucky—we were all in the big lounge, and there was this sudden absolute stillness. Somewhere far away a dog howled, and Brian Wilson says that's when he knew what was going to happen. He'd been in an earthquake near Cape Town, years ago, and he remembered that stillness. He just yelled to us all to get outside, we grabbed the children, and just as we got out there was this heaving feeling, and—well, we saw the roof collapse then.'

Julie went back inside, to find that the two doctors were putting a splint on a broken leg—the man Julie had seen being carried down the hill.

'Really should be reduced,' David said to Rob.

'I know,' Rob agreed. 'We can splint now to immobilise, and see that he's one of the first to be taken away when the helicopter comes from Umtata.'

They were working together with no problems, Julie realised—all their differences, all their hostility had disappeared when they were faced with the challenge of what had to be done.

'Still no telephone connection?' Rob asked, and David shook his head.

'Someone must know, somewhere, what's happened,' he said. 'The Met people will surely be tracing where the most damage is—they'll fly us in some help sooner or later.' He glanced around. 'How are we doing?'

'Pretty well,' Rob said. 'How about these burns, Julie—do you need any help with them?'

Julie shook her head. 'We've almost finished,' she said, and she handed Sarah another packet of tubular mesh overdressing, to hold the gauze covering in place.

'But we could do with more silver sulfadiazine,' Sarah told them. 'We've almost finished what we have.'

Rob straightened, and came over to them. 'Use cerium nitrate solution in a wet soak,' he suggested. 'I'll go and see how much of it we have.'

Sometimes, through the long day, they stopped long enough to drink a mug of tea, then got back to work again.

In the late afternoon, two helicopters came from Umtata. A doctor and two nurses were there, and the most seriously wounded people were taken to hospital. There had been other settlements more badly affected, the weary doctor told them, and they had been kept busy from early morning until now. But they had brought food, and medical supplies, and they also brought news that the telephone lines were being repaired.

'If it can be arranged, we'll come back tomorrow or the next day, and bring you more food, and more drugs and bandages,' the doctor promised them. He looked around. 'Meanwhile, you'll have to do the best you can—

makeshift beds on the veranda. Tomorrow, send anyone who's able to go back to start work on repairing the huts.'

Soon after the two helicopters had left, one of the mothers from the maternity ward came in search of Julie, and she hurried off, knowing that Patience would have waited as long as possible before sending for her.

It was a straightforward birth, though, and within ten minutes Julie put a perfect baby girl into her mother's arms. In spite of what she had said to the mother, she had been worried about the baby's size, with four weeks still to go to the due date, but she could see, even before Patience confirmed the weight at almost seven pounds, that the baby was all right.

'Where is your husband?' she asked the young mother.

'His arm was hurt when the hut fell,' the girl told her. 'After he brought me here, he went to wait for the doctor.'

Leaving mother and baby in Patience's care, Julie went back to the general ward, where she asked Agnes Nguli to find someone to look for the father.

'I know him,' Agnes told her. 'He has a dislocated shoulder—Dr Shaw put a sling on him. I will find him, Julie, and send him to see his wife and his child.'

Rob was finishing bandaging a woman with bad burns, and Julie could see that he needed someone to pass bandages and clips to him. She moved in beside him, and gave him the dressing he needed.

'Thanks,' he said. 'Where have you been?'

'Delivering a baby,' she told him.

'Oh. Well, I suppose that was something that wouldn't wait,' he agreed. For a moment his eyes held hers, and he smiled, a slow, tired smile, but as Julie smiled back the world narrowed to the two of them, and this sweet closeness between them. Only for a moment, because there was still so much to be done, so many people to care for. But Julie went back to work with her heart warm, and some of her weariness gone.

At last there was no more bandaging to be done, no more burns to be tended to, and everyone had been given tea. The kitchen staff were doing their best to organise a huge pot of soup and some bread, and then they would have to be settled for the night.

'We need more blankets,' Rob said worriedly and ran his hand through his already untidy dark hair.

'There are plenty of blankets up at the mission station,' Steve Winter told him. 'In the bedroom section, and it isn't damaged. We'll take the Land Rover and see what we can bring back.'

Rob helped Julie up, then Meg said she would come too, to get some more clothes for the children. Little Faith, seeing her mother climb into the Land Rover, began to cry.

'Let her come,' said her father, and Sarah lifted Faith up.

The bedroom wing was undamaged, and they loaded into the Land Rover as many blankets as possible. Meg filled a suitcase with clothes for the children. Little Faith, obviously tired and sleepy now, was set down on a blanket beside the Land Rover as they worked.

'That should do it,' Rob said at last. 'I don't think we can fit in any more, but we can come back up tomorrow.' He looked up, and his voice changed. 'Faith—come back!' he called.

The little girl was running purposefully towards the rubble that had been the big lounge of the mission station. For a moment, it seemed to Julie when she thought about it later, they were all frozen as Faith reached the archway, and the door hanging drunkenly on broken hinges. Then Rob and Steve both began to run.

But they were too late, for as the child reached the broken doorway the touch of her small feet on the unstable ruined structure must have been all that was needed. The heavy wooden door collapsed on top of the little girl.

Meg screamed, a high, thin, despairing scream. But before anyone could move Rob turned round.

'Stay where you are,' he told them. 'We dare not risk any other movement. Now, Steve—move slowly.'

Meg and Julie, motionless, watched and waited. Moving an inch at a time, Rob and Steve reached the fallen door. Slowly, with infinite care, they eased it up. Once the stone pillar near by seemed to shudder, but it didn't fall. Rob was holding the door now, and Steve was bending down. Julie, sick at heart, found that Meg's hand was grasping her arm.

'Lift her out, Steve,' Rob said. 'It's all right, I've got it.'

The door must have been very heavy, and he could only ease it up a little. Steve Winter lay down flat, and in a few moments he was easing backwards, carrying Faith in his arms.

And Faith, incredibly, was crying. Crying so loudly that she couldn't be badly hurt, Julie realised. With a stifled sob, Meg ran towards her husband and her little girl.

But Julie's eyes were on Rob, as he eased the door down again. He dared not let it go down too quickly, she could see. All around him there were broken walls, hanging roof rafters, and it could all fall in on him if there was any sudden movement.

Meg had taken Faith in her arms, but Julie, hearing her sudden indrawn breath, knew she had just realised the danger Rob was in.

And then, unbelievably, Rob had managed to ease the heavy door down again and was backing away, slowly, carefully.

'It's all right—Julie, it's all right,' Meg said unevenly. 'He's safe.'

Julie went towards him then, and he took both her hands in his. Neither of them said anything for a long time.

'If your face wasn't so dirty,' Rob said at last, not quite steadily, 'I might think you were a ghost.'

'I thought were going to be one,' Julie replied.

He released her hands and turned to Meg, who had Faith in her arms, holding her as if she would never let her go.

'I doubt if I'll ever hear a sound as welcome as this child bawling!' he said.

'Why wasn't she crushed by the door?' asked Meg. 'It—looked as if it fell right on top of her.'

'There was a hole torn in the floor,' Steve told her. He was very white too, Julie saw now. 'She'd fallen into that. She was—very lucky.' His voice stern now, he turned to the child. 'Faith, why did you go over there? I told you to stay right here.'

Faith had stopped crying now. There was a graze down one chubby little cheek, but miraculously that was all. 'I wanted mine baby,' she said.

Silently, Meg produced the baby doll Faith had been given when Robin was born. 'Your baby was in your cot,' she told the child.

With a cry of joy, Faith took her doll and held it close.

'Let's get back down the hill,' Steve said.

By the time they got back, everyone had been given hot soup and some bread, and Sarah and Agnes were doing what they could to settle people for the night.

'Thank goodness for these blankets,' Sarah said when they unloaded the Land Rover. 'It isn't really cold, but most of them are suffering from shock, and they do need a blanket.'

Rob joined David in doing final rounds of the little hospital—bursting at the seams now, with patients in every room, even the dining-room.

'I'd like to get the children off to bed,' Sarah said to Julie, and when David and Rob came back to the office, the only room left empty now, she said she thought she would go up to the cottage if she wasn't needed here.

'I'll come with you,' David said, 'and help to get the children to bed. If that's all right with you, Rob?'

'Sure,' Rob replied. 'I'll be around.'

'If you need me, send someone for me,' David told him.

'I'll do that,' Rob promised.

It was a strange feeling, Julie thought, watching David and Sarah go off with their children, just as they had the night of the party. Once again Clare was in David's arms, almost asleep, and Timothy stumbled with weariness. But all four of them were dirty and exhausted now, as they walked up the path to the cottage.

She turned and found Rob watching her. And he, she realised, was exhausted too.

'When did you last have something to eat, or a cup of coffee?' she asked him, and the emotion that suddenly and treacherously tightened her throat made her speak severely.

'I can't remember,' Rob admitted.

'Sit down,' she told him, 'and put your feet up. I'll go and get some coffee, and there should be some of the sandwiches left in the picnic basket.'

The Wild Coast and their time there seemed like a lifetime ago, she thought, as she waited for the kettle to boil and found a cheese roll for Rob.

She made coffee for both of them, and went back through.

At the doorway, she stopped. Rob had fallen asleep,

sitting at the desk. He hadn't had time to shave before they left that morning, and his chin was dark. There was a streak of grime down one cheek, his dark hair was untidy, and there was dust in it from the fallen mission buildings. He looked dreadful.

And she loved him with all her heart. She knew that with complete certainty now, and she wondered how she could ever have doubted this. He was her love, now and always.

He opened his eyes.

'I—brought you coffee,' she said, with difficulty.

'Come here,' he said to her.

'And a cheese roll,' Julie told him.

He smiled. 'Come here,' he said again, and held out his arms to her.

Carefully she put the coffee-cups and the cheese roll down on the desk. Then she went into his arms.

He held her close to him. 'Don't you be thinking, girl dear, that you will ever get away from me again,' he murmured, and his lips were against her hair.

She leaned against him. 'And don't you be thinking that I will ever want to,' she told him.

There was a moment's surprised silence, and then he laughed, his dark head thrown back. And then, when he stopped laughing, he kissed her.

Or perhaps, Julie thought, she kissed him. It didn't really matter. There was no time, then, for all the things that had to be said. They would have to wait.

She was still in Rob's arms when Agnes Nguli came to the door—showing no surprise at all at finding them like that—and said that one of the patients had pulled his drip out.

'I have set it up again,' she said, 'but I think he should be sedated—he's very restless, and he is making the other patients restless too.'

'I'll come and have a look at him,' said Rob.

'Thank you, Dr Kennedy,' the big sister replied formally, and spoiled the effect by smiling widely, and with obvious delight, at both of them.

Much as they all needed to sleep, it was never possible for more than an hour or two at a time, for there was always someone needing attention. But by the next day, when many people could be sent back to their huts to begin to rebuild, things were much quieter and more orderly. Later that day, the helicopter came back from the State hospital, and took some more patients away.

Even so, it was the end of the week before the small hospital was functioning more or less as normal. The damage throughout the country had been surprisingly little, and limited to a belt which included the mission station, the settlements closest to it, and a small town further north. The hospital itself, so close to the mission station, had been incredibly fortunate, but similar things had happened, they found, in other earthquakes—sometimes two buildings almost side by side, one reduced to rubble and the other left intact.

And at last it was possible to think of themselves.

'I've known for so long that it was you I'd been waiting for,' Rob told Julie as they sat under the big tree beside the river, when the sun had just gone down and the heat of the day had cooled.

'But you never said—I didn't know,' Julie replied, her head on his shoulder.

'You must have known,' he insisted. 'Sure and I think almost every other person in the hospital knew!'

Julie smiled. 'Maybe they did, but I didn't,' she countered.

He turned her head towards him and kissed her. 'Well, you know now, and that's all that matters,' he told her when they drew apart.

The day after that, Sarah and the children left to fly back to Durban, David taking them through to Umtata.

'But Daddy's coming home soon,' Timothy told Julie. 'Just as soon as he can get another doctor to come here.'

'That will be nice for all of you,' Julie said.

'Yes, it will,' Timothy agreed.

'Specially for Tiger,' Clare put in, obviously feeling she had been out of the conversation too long. 'Tiger will be very happy, he likes us all to be together.'

And so do you, Julie thought, and she bent and hugged the little girl. 'I'm sure Tiger will be happy,' she agreed.

Clare looked up at her. 'Are you and Rob going to get married, Julie? Are you going to wear a white dress, and have a long veil?'

'I suppose so,' Julie replied. 'We haven't thought about the details yet, but—yes, I'm sure I will.'

Clare sighed deeply. 'I love weddings,' she said. She looked at Julie, unblinking. 'My best friend Jilly was a flower-girl when her big sister got married. You should have seen her dress, it was lovely!'

For a moment, above her head, Julie's eyes met Sarah's, and a question was asked and answered.

'Well, now, I was wondering,' Julie said casually, 'if you might like to be my flower-girl, Clare.'

Clare's small face became pink with delight. 'Yes, I'd like that very much,' she said gravely. And then, excitement bursting out, 'Can I go and tell Patience? And Mummy, do I have time to go up and tell Meg?'

'Tell Patience, but you'll have to leave Julie to tell Meg,' her mother told her. 'Daddy has our suitcases in, and we have to be on our way.'

When the Land Rover was out of sight, Julie turned to Rob and told him that Clare was going to be her flower-girl.

'Do you mind?' she asked him.

They were both in uniform, so he didn't take her in his arms. But his hand closed on hers for a moment.

'Mind?' he said. 'Girl dear, if I did need anything to convince me that you had no regrets, this would be it.' He smiled down at her. 'And in any case I'm just so happy that we are to be married that you can have Agnes Nguli for your bridesmaid if you want!'

From the time of the earthquake, Rob and David had worked together much more harmoniously, but when the news came that David would be able to leave, because a young doctor from the big hospital in Johannesburg was to come, Rob admitted to Julie that he was pleased.

'We never did get on too well,' he admitted, 'right from the start. And of course, after you came, it was much worse. Oh, I'll admit a great deal of it was my fault, for I am not the most patient and forbearing of men, as you will find out.'

'I didn't think you were,' Julie returned, unable to suppress the amusement she felt at this.

A fortnight later, David left. Steve Winter had to go to Umtata, so he took him through, and they left early in the morning, making any goodbyes very quick.

But Julie felt nothing—other than, she had to admit, some relief—when she said goodbye. At long last, David was nothing more than a doctor she had once known, once been in love with. Part of yesterday, she thought, while Rob was all of her today and her tomorrows.

The new doctor, Jake Marais, arrived a few days later. He was young and enthusiastic, but at the same time he made it obvious that he wanted to learn all he could from Rob, from Julie, from the rest of the staff.

'We'll get on fine,' Rob assured Julie. 'We'll work well together.'

Rebuilding had started on the mission station.

It was strange, Steve Winter said to them, that it had

been so very hard to get any funds for their mission work before this, but somehow the earthquake, and the fact that half of the mission station had been destroyed, seemed to have touched people's imagination—and their pockets—and there were generous donations. A temporary prefabricated building had even been sent, so that they still had a community centre and a place for the women to do their weaving.

Letters flew between Tabanduli and Cape Town, and soon letters weren't enough for Julie's mother, and there were excited phone calls as the plans for the wedding took form.

'I wish Rob's folks could come,' she said to Julie on one phone call. 'We could easily put them up, you know that.'

'I know, Mum,' Julie replied. 'But Rob's mother hasn't been too well, and it's a long way. And Rob has promised them that next year we'll go over for a proper holiday with them.'

Her mother was off on another tack now. 'Are you sure you can't manage more than a week before the wedding?' she asked worriedly. 'The reception's all organised, but I just hope your dress will be all right. Miss Read is working from your sketch, and your measurements, but——'

'It will be fine, Mum,' Julie assured her.

Young Jake Marais was doing well, and learning fast, but Rob felt it wasn't fair to leave him for long on his own. So Rob would arrive in Cape Town only the day before the wedding, and he had promised that a week later they would be back at the hospital.

'Only a short honeymoon, I'm afraid,' he said to Julie. 'But we'll make up for that next year, when I take you to Ireland.'

'Where are we going for our honeymoon?' Julie asked him. 'I need to know what clothes to take.'

He shook his head. 'All you need to know, girl dear, is to take a bathing-costume, or maybe two, and a dress or two. That should do you fine.'

And more than that he refused to say.

The night before Julie was to fly to Cape Town, there was a special dinner organised by Agnes Nguli and Meg Winter, but again held at the hospital so that as many people as possible could be there.

'And now,' Meg said, when the coffee-cups were cleared away, 'we want to give you your wedding present. It's a joint one, from the staff here and from all of us up at the mission, and you have to follow us to get it.'

She led the way out of the dining-room, and up the path to the cottage David and Sarah had been in, which was now to be Rob's and Julie's. There had been no time to do much to it, but Julie had promised herself that when they came back she would brighten it up, and make it a real home for them—their first home.

'You can go in,' Meg said, opening the door.

Rob, with Julie's hand in his, went into the cottage.

Julie, following him, looked around, disbelieving. There were new curtains at the windows—soft kingfisher woven curtains, and the clear bright colour was picked up again in two handwoven rugs on the floor.

'This is our present?' she asked, overcome.

Meg nodded, her eyes bright with excitement. 'I knew you liked this colour,' she said, 'and we've been working hard to get it finished in time. Do you like it?'

Julie could barely speak. 'I love it,' she said at last. 'It's just what I would have chosen, and it's going to be so lovely, coming to live here.'

It was, she thought, just the most perfect present, specially woven for them for their first home. Monika

Jansen took some photographs, and then gave Julie the spool to take with her.

'So that your mother can see how it looks,' she explained.

'Thank you, Monika, it was so kind of you to think of that,' Julie said. She hesitated, but only for a moment, then she hugged the German nurse.

'Such foolishness!' Monika said severely, but she was pink with pleasure, as Julie turned to Elsa Braun, and then to Agnes Nguli, and to Patience, and the others from the mission station.

The next day Rob took her to Umtata, to the airport where he had met her all those months ago. Parting was bearable, because he would soon join her for their wedding.

And the last few days before the wedding flew by. Sarah, with Timothy and Clare, arrived the day before, bringing Clare's dress, which Sarah had made. And bringing, too, David's excuses.

'He's just started this new job at the hospital,' Sarah explained, 'and it really wouldn't be fair to come away, even for a few days. But he specially said I was to wish you and Rob every happiness.'

Rob himself arrived later the same day, and Julie drove out to the airport to meet him, wanting this little while just for the two of them, before the busyness of the wedding caught them up.

'But the mountain is beautiful,' Rob said, as they drove towards it.

'It is, isn't it?' Julie agreed. 'I've lived in sight of Table Mountain for most of my life, and I miss it terribly when I'm away.'

He glanced at her. 'And do you think, now,' he asked her gravely, 'that being married to me will help to make up for the missing of Table Mountain?'

'I think it might,' Julie replied, just as gravely. And then they both had to laugh, and she found herself thinking that one of the special things was their shared laughter.

The last few weeks had been so busy, in the hospital and making long-distance arrangements for the wedding, that somehow, she realised the next day, she hadn't thought too much about the wedding itself, she had gone happily along with her mother's arrangements. Marrying Rob, being his wife—that was more important than the actual wedding-day, she had somehow thought.

But now the day was here, and she realised that it did matter, it was important.

She rose early and went out into the garden. Everything was still and silent, and her beloved Table Mountain rose into the sky, already a deep blue.

Today, she thought with wonder, is my wedding-day. Today Rob and I are to be married.

Rob had spent the night with her brother in his flat, and she wouldn't see him until they met in church. She had smiled a little at her mother's insistence on that, but now it seemed right, and conforming to custom seemed part of the pattern of the day.

Tess, the old golden Labrador, woke then, and came out to meet her and lead her back to the kitchen for the ritual morning biscuit.

'Julie!' her mother exclaimed, surprised. 'I was just going to bring you breakfast in bed.'

Julie shook her head. 'I don't want breakfast in bed, I want breakfast here in the kitchen, with you and Dad.'

Her mother smiled. 'And Sarah and Clare and Timothy,' she pointed out, for they were staying. She hesitated, then said, too casually, 'It's a pity Sarah's husband couldn't come, isn't it?'

Julie hadn't been sure, until now, that her mother remembered, that she had realised who David Shaw was.

'It doesn't matter one way or the other, Mum,' she said quietly. 'Ten years is a long time, David is happily married, and Rob and I love each other.'

Her mother hugged her. 'I know that, dear,' she said shakily. 'And I love him, and he and your dad get on well together, and—oh, Julie, I'm so happy!' And she burst into tears.

'Why is your mummy crying, Julie?' Clare asked, coming into the kitchen.

'Because she's happy,' Julie told her. 'Sometimes grown-up people do that, Clare.'

'I smile when I'm happy,' Clare said definitely. 'When can I put my dress on, Julie?'

'Not for quite a while,' Julie told her. 'The wedding is at twelve, and I'm going out soon to have my hair done, and then my friend Barbara will come, and she'll put on her bridesmaid's dress, and you'll put on yours, and I'll put on my dress and my veil.'

'Yours is the prettiest of all,' Clare said generously. And then, thinking about it, 'But mine is very pretty too, and so is Barbara's.'

Clare and Barbara were in dresses of deep rose, because this was a summer wedding, and the contrast with the ivory of Julie's dress was just what Julie had hoped for.

Suddenly, it seemed, the time had flown by, and they were arriving at the little stone church close to Julie's home. Clare, very conscious of her responsibilities, lifted the train of Julie's dress carefully, as Julie's father smiled down at her and gave her his arm.

The small church was full of people, but there was only a moment when Julie was conscious of the friendly, smiling faces. Then there was only Rob, waiting for her, his dark blue eyes smiling down as he took her hand in his, his voice deep and strong as he repeated the familiar and yet suddenly new words of the marriage service.

Then they had exchanged rings, and the minister was proclaiming that they were man and wife, and telling Rob that he could kiss the bride.

Outside, the sun shone from a clear blue sky, and they were surrounded by friends and relatives. Clare handed out little boxes of confetti, and Timothy, who had maintained that he didn't want to do any silly things like that, changed his mind and helped.

Then there were photographs in the lovely grounds of the country club, and there was the lunchtime reception, and champagne, and dancing, and the wedding-cake, and the toasts, and her mother and father hugging her as she and Rob said goodbye and slipped away.

'Alone at last!' Rob said as they got into her brother's car. 'Sure and I thought the day would never end! But it was a lovely wedding,' he added hastily.

Julie looked down at the shining gold of her wedding-ring. 'It was, wasn't it?' she agreed. She looked at him. 'But I'm glad it's over, Rob.'

'So am I,' Rob said, with heartfelt agreement.

'Well, I can see we're heading for the airport,' Julie said, 'but what are we to do with the car?'

'No problem,' he assured her. 'My new brother-in-law says he'll get someone to take him out later to pick it up.'

A couple of bathing-costumes, and a dress or two, he had said she would need. Julie began to wonder, and to hope. And when they left the plane at East London, and transferred to a very small plane, she knew she was right. Half an hour later they landed on the airstrip beside Seacrest, on the Wild Coast.

'I couldn't think of anywhere nicer for a honeymoon,' Rob said, as they walked down towards the thatched rondavels of the hotel.

'Neither can I,' Julie assured him. 'I was hoping we were coming here.'

He took her hand in his. 'Only one change,' he told her. 'This time we have the honeymoon suite.'

The small rondavel was exactly the same as the ones they had had before, except that it had a double bed.

'Mrs Kennedy, you are blushing!' Rob said, delighted.

'I'm not,' Julie denied.

He looked down at her, and now the laughter was gone. 'I'm not going to carry you over the threshold, girl dear,' he said softly, 'for I am keeping that for when we get back to our own cottage, at the hospital, at the end of the week.'

He took her hand, and they went into the little thatched hut. Outside, the golden sand dropped away to the deep blue of the sea. It was a perfect place for a honeymoon.

And when the honeymoon was over they would go back to their work at the mission hospital, Julie thought with deep satisfaction. The mission hospital, and the beginning of their life together.

'Thank you for coming into my life, Dr Kennedy,' she said, not quite steadily.

And she stood on tiptoe, and kissed her husband.

— MEDICAL ♥ROMANCE —

The books for your enjoyment this month are:

A DREAM WORTH SHARING Hazel Fisher
GIVE BACK THE YEARS Elisabeth Scott
UNCERTAIN FUTURE Angela Devine
REPEAT PRESCRIPTION Sonia Deane

♥ ♥ ♥ ♥ ♥

Treats in store!

Watch next month for the following absorbing stories:

CARIBBEAN TEMPTATION Jenny Ashe
A PRACTICAL MARRIAGE Lilian Darcy
AN UNEXPECTED AFFAIR Laura MacDonald
SURGEON'S DAUGHTER Drusilla Douglas

Available from Boots, Martins, John Menzies, W.H. Smith, Woolworths and other paperback stockists.

Also available from Mills and Boon Reader Service, P.O. Box 236, Thornton Road, Croydon, Surrey CR9 3RU.

Readers in South Africa — write to:
Independent Book Services Pty, Postbag X3010, Randburg, 2125, S. Africa.